Bloodletting
By J.R. Curtis

Prologue

There is something to be said about the cold that the Jacobs-Clanton handcart company endured. Though, none could ever confirm they had actually met a survivor of the unfortunate journey, many could recall the winter that it took place in.

A mean, vengeful winter that hardly any would dispute was rivaled. Frostbite practically waited just outside, for any that were foolhardy enough to venture out on a windy day. A touch of sniffles or a cough could become a death sentence for any that could not warm their home constantly.

Eggs in the chicken coop swelled and cracked open, the frozen embryos inside pushing their way out in a bitter mockery of birth. The teats of milk cows were blistered and blackened with infection brought on by the relentless freeze.

By the time folk pulled themselves from their homes and out into town the following spring, there were far fewer neighbors than when winter began.

Those that had survived, were left with scarred-over tissue on their faces, a memento from the bitter winter air. Others were missing fingers, limbs, and the light in their eyes.

So when folk learned that the forlorn handcart company had never reached their destination, not many thought twice.

Chapter 1

In the frozen forest of the untamed wilderness, The Jacobs-Clanton handcart company had finally stopped. Though they had fought valiantly through tall drifts and icy rivers for days, the snow had, at last, brought them to a halt.

It was a pitiful and bleak scene. Fear hung heavy in the air like a dense fog, as these pioneers went about the work of setting up camp. As tents were erected and wagons circled, these unfortunate souls cast looks to each other through downcast eyes.

Husbands looked to Wives, Fathers and Mothers to Children, and Leaders to their flock. Heavy, hopeless looks of complete uncertainty and desperation. The somber affair, backlit by cries of hungry babies and the gloomy light of the falling snow, illustrated the perfect portrait of human suffering.

Spirits were not just low, they were buried six feet deep.

Across the camp, in one of the larger tents that had been erected, one of the leaders of the expedition had begun to breathe his final breaths.

Mr. Jacobs, normally an example of health and strength, was quickly losing his battle with pneumonia. At his side was his business partner and pastor; Father Clanton.

Clanton dabbed away the drool from the dying man's lips. He reassured and soothed their nearly comatose leader as he held a cold rag to his feverish head.

But then, mere moments later, Jacobs departed the world with the soft hiss of a death rattle.

Clanton hung his head, though tears did not come. Jacobs had been near death for a week now. If anything, his passing had brought peace to Clanton as he watched his friend be finally relieved of his suffering.

Taking a moment to compose himself and briefly mourn, Clanton stood up and walked through the flap of the tent.

Outside, he looked to Caleb; a young man with a kind disposition but still with a fire for mischief and games. He was a hard worker and was known around the camp and well liked.

"Caleb." Clanton called out to him.

Caleb turned from the task he was assisting another with. "Yes?" He asked.

"Mr. Jacobs has died." Clanton said quietly, keeping his tone muted enough to slow the news that would soon wash over the camp like an avalanche. "Fetch Mr. Mercer."

Caleb stepped away from his work and nodded. He turned and walked toward the other side of camp.

On an icy rock at the edge of the circle of handcarts, Abraham Mercer sat. In his gloved hand he held a weathered tintype-photograph of his recently departed wife. The photo had been taken just before they had embarked on this journey. Abraham held Laura around her waist as they both smiled. He smiled sadly at her cheery expression in the photo, an expression he would never see again in life.

Still well within a heavy quilt of grief, freezing tears rolled down Abraham's face as he looked upon it.

"I'm sorry." He muttered softly before stuffing the photo back into his coat.

It was then that he noticed Caleb standing before him. Abraham hurriedly composed himself and wiped his eyes before addressing the young man.

"What is it Caleb?" He asked, slightly embarrassed with his head low.

"Father Clanton has requested of you Abraham." Caleb informed him. "Jacobs has died."

Abraham took this news well. Jacobs' death had been hovering over them all for weeks. He let out a breath, knowing already what the old preacher wanted.

"He did, did he?" Abraham replied back. "Well, let's go see what that old bible thumper wants."

Abraham stood, dusted off the snow from his trousers and walked to join Caleb. He placed a hand on the boy's shoulder and patted it, letting him lead.

As Caleb and Abraham crossed the camp to go rendezvous with Father Clanton, another member of the camp had begun to eye them curiously.

Mr. Buchanan, stood next to a small cart and chewed on a hunk of salted pork. He had sat back and observed the bustling camp as the lodgings were prepared. His age, though not elderly, was old enough that his unhelpful nature in regard to manual labor was not scorned, and Buchanan was glad for it. But now, his attention had turned elsewhere.

He'd watched as the boy emerged from Jacobs' tent and gone to fetch Mr. Mercer. But his interest had risen as Caleb quickly led Abraham back to where he had just come from.

As he watched them, he developed an assumption to himself, and was correct. He figured Jacob's had finally croaked and Mr. Mercer had drawn the bad lot of being his replacement.

He grinned a little bit to himself at this thought, Abraham was a decent man, but no leader.

He watched as the two men disappeared into the tent and thought again on the proposal he was silently developing.

Buchanan had just returned from a scouting mission. As he had walked ahead, in search of a break in the snow and the massive drifts, he had briefly considered abandoning the group entirely. The situation had gone from bleak to dire rather quickly, and he was reluctant to stick around with all of these; panicked pilgrims he regarded as "dead weight".

Mr. Buchanan, a retired bounty hunter and an all around rough character, had only been hired for his suspicious demeanor and speed with a gun. Though he didn't much care what became of this outfit, he was, however, interested in the secret meeting that was being held in Jacobs' tent.

He spit out a hunk of gristle before walking toward the gathering to join in.

Back in the dead man's tent, Abraham and Clanton were in the midst of an argument.

"I don't know father." Abraham spoke.

Clanton raised his arms in beseechment as he continued. "Oh come on Abe. Most of the flock already look to you for leadership." Clanton stuttered as he tried to find the right words. "This would be merely a formality."

Abraham raised a hand in protest. "Oh it is much more than that Father."

Clanton furrowed a brow. "Why?" He asked desperately. "Jacobs is gone...They need to have someone to...to follow! A plan!" Clanton continued to press.

Abraham had grown silent, trying to end the discussion.

"Abe they need you-" Clanton had continued before being interrupted by an outburst from Abraham.

"I will not be the one to guide these people to the grave!" Abraham shot back angrily.

Clanton, though surprised, scowled and brought a finger to his lips. "Lower your voice!" He hissed.

Abraham spit forth his next words in an angry whisper. "Look outside!" He spoke in a hushed crescendo. "We are marooned here. One by one these people will starve. Their pleading eyes will find mine and they will look to me as they fight the call to die."

Clanton's gaze fell in defeat as Abraham spoke. But then, movement at the door pulled his attention elsewhere.

"What news Mr. Buchanan?" He asked.

Buchanan, now standing just inside the tent, shrugged. "I walked at least a mile." He spoke. "Snowdrifts are far too high for any cart to leave anytime soon."

Clanton sighed and moved to sit in a chair opposite Jacob's bed. He rifled through his medical kit and pulled forth a small bottle of whiskey.

Abraham watched Clanton sadly, he couldn't recall ever seeing the old preacher with a bottle in his hand before.

Clanton spoke as he uncorked it. "Then perhaps you are right Abraham." Clanton paused and drank deeply before continuing. "May God help us all."

The atmosphere of the tent, heavy and depressing, hung silent for moments. Then, Buchanan spoke again.

"You know." He started. "Walking around out there has brung me a sense of familiarity. I believe I've been up this way once before." Buchanan mused.

"You didn't think to mention this?" Abraham interjected with cocked eyebrows.

Buchanan shrugged dismissively. "Well I knew I had been in the general area." Buchanan said as he strode to Clanton's side and took the bottle of whiskey for himself. After a gulp of the spirits he spoke again. "But now that I've had the chance to find my bearings...I've been on this exact trail before."

Buchanan then polished off the whiskey and tossed the bottle into Clanton's lap. "Back when I was still chasing bounties...I recall an old army fort a few miles from here." Buchan continued, accompanied by a half-belch, half-hiccup from the alcohol.

Clanton's spirits immediately rose, and he shot up rapidly from the chair he sat in. "Do you think it is still there?" Clanton demanded of Buchanan.

Buchanan raised his shoulders indifferently. "Hard to say. 'Twas a long time ago now. Could just as well be abandoned."

Clanton's voice sped, ever excited by the possibilities that populated his brain. "Could you travel ahead? Send aid when you reach them?" He stammered out excitedly.

Buchanan squinted in quiet thought. "Perhaps. It is little more than a pipe dream at the moment however." He said gruffly.

"Abraham will accompany you!" Clanton burst out.

"I will?" Abraham asked, shooting a look of annoyance at Clanton.

Clanton looked back at Abraham, his eyes focused in a serious gaze. "Yes." Clanton replied.

Abraham stared back at Clanton, a slight scowl hanging on his face. He thought for a moment but shook his head at any retort his mind conjured.

"It appears I will." Abraham said with a sigh.

Buchanan raised an eyebrow cautiously before speaking. "This is injun country fellas. Ain't no walk down to the fishing hole with a lunch basket. You sure you can manage Mr. Mercer?"

"I can." Abraham assured him, his gaze still fixed on Clanton. "Or else I wouldn't have volunteered so eagerly."

Clanton ignored Abraham, his thoughts elsewhere, thinking on the plan as the men discussed it around him.

"I will accompany you as well." Caleb interjected, breaking the silence he'd held up until then. He walked up eagerly from his post at the far side of the tent. His voice was excited and full of the young bullheadedness that was to be expected at his age.

Abraham broke his gaze from Clanton and turned to Caleb, a hand already raised in protest. "That might not be the best idea." Abraham said dismissively.

Caleb talked over him with fervor, his words leaving his mouth as fast as his mind could build them. "You ain't gonna find anyone else!" He protested. "The rest of the men have families, children. We all got nobody, we're all there is."

This last phrase visibly pained Abraham, the loss of his wife still stung fresh, new even.

Caleb noticed the pain that speaking so rashly had caused, almost immediately. Embarrassed, he cast his eyes upon the floor and grew quiet.

Buchanan broke up the silence with a loud snort of mucous before spitting it onto the ground. "Well boy." He spoke as he wiped the spittle from his lips. "I suppose as long as you don't slow us, you're welcome to tag along."

Caleb beamed.

Clanton looked to the three men, exasperated solace filling his face. "Then it is settled." He stated. "I'll have some of the women gather up what provisions we can spare. You men get yourselves prepared as you need." Clanton then hurried away to the opening of the tent. Just before exiting, he turned around once more to the men. "Thank you all." He said. "I will pray every moment that this endeavor is successful."

News of the trek to the old army fort had spread around the camp so rapidly, that Abraham had had his hand shaken and been wished well so many times he couldn't count. All of this occurred before he had even returned to his bag to collect it.

This camp that until moments ago had seemed so hopeless, now buzzed with this newfound iota of hope. The chances were slim and no one would deny it, but they clung to this new possibility with everything they had.

For the first time that any of them could recently recall, the camp was lively, happy even.

But, as the night wore on and bags were packed, goodbyes were said and the men vanished forward into the night.

Then, once again, all was quiet around the camp.

Left only to wait and hope, the remaining members of the Jacobs-Clanton handcart company returned to their meager duties and desperate reality, praying for a better tomorrow.

Chapter 2

Gently, Abraham wafted soft breaths onto the glowing tinder. Methodically stoking it, he eyed every blossoming flame with admiration and discipline. Squinting through wispy smoke that caused his eyes to weep, he finally saw the meager flames catch the large tinder. He sat back proudly as the fire grew steadily.

Abraham stood and walked a few steps backward to join Mr. Buchanan and Caleb who sat on rocks near the fire.

Mr. Buchanan, gloves held tightly in his gritted teeth, expertly rolled a cigarette with freezing bare hands.

Caleb, adjacent to him, watched the man with curious intention.

The old gunfighter, after placing his completed smoke between his lips and lighting it, noticed the hanging gaze of the young man.

"Do you suffer from a lazy eye son?" Buchanan asked gruffly.

Caleb's eyes dropped to the snow, embarrassed. "No sir." He offered back meekly.

Buchanan raised an eyebrow as he puffed on the tobacco. "No?" He grumbled with a joking half-chuckle.

"Well, there must be something about my appearance that catches your fancy then?"

Caleb grew scarlet, his eyes lowering even more. "No that isn't it sir." He said back.

Mr. Buchanan grinned slightly. "Well then speak up boy! Leave silence for the dead."

Caleb cautiously raised his gaze again to meet Buchanan's. "It's just..." Caleb started. "I heard some stories about you. From some of the men in camp I mean... Saying how you used to chase outlaws."

Buchanan drew again on his cigarette and offered back an understanding nod. "Ah. So you'd be after a campfire tale then." He said over an exhale of smoke.

"Well no." Caleb stammered for a moment. "I mean...yes. If you'd care to oblige sir."

Buchanan smiled. "You'd like to hear the tale of my gunfight with "Grinning" Everett DeShaw?" Buchanan asked loudly.

Caleb tried to reply but Buchanan continued, growing in volume and speaking rather aggressively. "Or perhaps the time I shared a drink with "Bloody" Homer Cox?"

This name caught Abraham's attention, who had otherwise not been paying mind to Caleb and Buchanan's conversation.

"You met "Bloody" Homer Cox?" Abraham asked, genuinely interested.

Buchanan ignored Abraham's interruption and continued his puzzling beratement of Caleb.

"Or maybe the many times I shot a man in the back before he ever saw me?" Buchanan asked, his eyes fiery and intense. "Or would you prefer to hear about my time with the railroad company? Is that it boy?"

Caleb began to shy away from Buchanan as much as he could, who continued nonetheless.

"And all the unspeakable things I did to the Indians therein?!" Buchanan nearly shouted.

"Alright." Abraham interjected sternly. "That's enough."

Buchanan did not heed him whatsoever, he only continued, growing louder and louder. "Or the women we butchered and the ones I watched my men rape?! The infants that we cast against rocks to save bullets?! The survivors that we marched until their feet bled?!"

"ENOUGH!" Abraham shouted over the belligerent man.

Buchanan silenced, scowling at Abraham a moment before composing himself and speaking again.

"The point being boy." Buchanan stated calmly and matter-of-factly. "The things I've done ain't meant for no dime-novels. Stories are one thing, and truth is another. I've done a whole lot of ugly and that's why I'm still alive. You best remember that."

Buchanan then stood, spitting a wad of phlegm into the fire with a sizzle. "How's that for a campfire tale?" He asked sourly, before departing to the nearby clearing to finish his cigarette.

Caleb and Abraham sat in near silence, the crackling of the fire their only respite from the discomfort.

"I'm sorry." Caleb spoke softly.

Abraham shook his head and turned to address the boy. "Pay him no mind Caleb. Do your best to put it out of your head."

Caleb thought quietly for a moment before speaking. "I didn't mean to anger him."

Abraham scoffed. "You didn't." He said, looking at Buchanan in the distance. "He's just a miserable old man at the end of his ill-perceived glory days. Anything can sound important coming from an elder's lips, no matter how foolish. Give him no regard."

Caleb chewed on this thought as Abraham stood to unpack his bedroll and stretch it out upon the ground.

"Go to sleep." Abraham instructed as he laid upon his bed. "We have much further to travel."

Chapter 3

Sometime during the night, Abraham stirred. As his eyes fluttered open in a languid fashion, he heard something. Something that he might describe as humming, but closer to the faint harmony of a choir.

Rising from his bedroll, he dusted the snowflakes from his clothes and panned his head this way and that. Eyes squinted, he tried to determine the source of the nearly angelic melody. A moon-like glow from behind some nearby trees proved to be the proper conclusion.

Abraham stood, bathed in the peculiar luminescence. Though such a phenomenon would normally frighten the one who witnessed it, Abraham himself was comforted. The light seemed to warm him, exuding an air of contentment from its concealed position.

With his boots softly crunching the snow beneath him as he walked, he moved toward the curious spectacle.

As he crossed the first line of trees toward the oddity, the melody grew in volume, but also in coherence.

It was a song. A song that Abraham himself recognized, something he could recall from many years ago, when he was only a boy.

Fear not God's lamb, for you aren't forgotten
Though the night hangs heavy and you fear the worst
I'll always return you to my side
I'll venture through, weather most cruel
And fiends and monsters most dreadful
I'll ford the river and cross the swamp
To find my little lamb once again

Fear not little soldier
All is not lost
As long as you fight til the end
And into the vastness of the night we shall venture
To do it all over again

Louder and clearer the melody grew until Abraham finally pushed through enough brush and limbs to see its source.

There, in a perfectly circular clearing was a woman. Clad in a white dress, she spun and danced slowly to the song as she sang. Her voice was angelic, her appearance awe inspiring. Though he didn't know why, tears began to form in the corners of Abraham's eyes.

Abraham looked on in wonder and shock as he took in the scene. The woman paid him no mind, not noticing him at all as she continued to sing and dance, emanating a heavenly glow. Long flowing hair cascaded down her back and bobbed to the rhythm her bare feet set upon the snow.

Meat; the smell of cooking meat pulled Abraham from this dream immediately.

Abraham's eyes shot open, above him, the gloomy sky of the early morning stared back. Smoke and steam wafted by his frozen nose and brought him up to a sitting position.

His companions sat next to the fire. Buchanan watched in anticipation as Caleb spun a spit over the flames; two rabbits skewered on the pole that rotated steadily. The audible sound of meat searing and fat cooking was tantalizing.

Buchanan, noticing that Abraham had awoken, turned to address him. "Can you believe it?" Buchanan shouted out. "The kids a natural! Shame it had to be rabbit, but it'll do."

Abraham's eyes widened in astonishment. "Where did you get that?" He asked Caleb, dumbfounded.

Caleb looked up from the spit, grinning. "Snared 'em about an hour ago." He spoke nonchalantly to cover the pride that burned in his chest. "Woke up and couldn't get back to sleep. Figured I'd go see what I could come up with."

Abraham rubbed his eyes, thinking surely he was still dreaming. "Well done." He congratulated Caleb with a nod.

Standing to join the men by the fire, the aroma of the cooking meat grew stronger and caused Abraham's stomach to growl. "Snares huh?" Abraham continued. "I never could get the hang of it."

Caleb shrugged. "Not much too it." He offered back with a sprinkle of earned ego.

Back on his seat, Buchanan smiled ear to ear as he watched the fat simmer on the rabbit. "Well praise to your daddy." He said happily. "Taught you well, sure enough."

Caleb scowled a little, not taking his attention from the cooking food. "No sir." He said. "It weren't that drunkard. That fella never taught me nothing, cept how to take a punch."

Buchanan, producing a cigarette from his coat, nodded knowingly. "I am familiar. Who taught you then?"

Caleb smiled to himself, thinking back on memories he hadn't explored in some time. He looked to Buchanan a moment before responding and quietly observed him. Though he did admire this man, he was still left a bit shaken after the outburst he had provided the night before.

"Well." Caleb started. "I run off soon as I could. Couple months later I got thrown in a boys home in one of them bigger cities."

Caleb leaned forward to peel a tiny piece of meat from the rabbit, and took a bite. Nodding to himself, he peeled two more pieces from the roast and handed them to Mr. Buchanan and Abraham.

Still chewing his food, Caleb continued. "After I couldn't take no more of that place, I run off again. Ended up running into a one legged trapper."

"A one legged trapper." Abraham said, amused and slightly chuckling.

"Yes sir." Caleb replied. "That's the truth. Lost it in the war he said."

Removing the rabbit from the spit, he handed it to Buchanan to divide up. Taking a knife from his side, Mr. Buchanan sliced the rabbit into three nearly equal pieces. He then passed two of them to Abraham and Caleb.

Caleb shoved the hunk of meat into his mouth greedily, the juices causing his cheeks to sting and contract from the flavor. He grinned to himself as he enjoyed the first real food he'd had in days.

"Well." Caleb said, as he swallowed the rabbit. "Circumstance put me in that old fellas' debt."

"Circumstance." Buchanan laughed. "You tried to rob him didn't you?"

Caleb chuckled back, a little nervous. "Just some of his dried meat. He was a big ole bastard. I figured he weren't gonna miss it."

Buchanan chuckled a little and nodded knowingly. As callous as he was, he had begun to like the kid. He reminded him of himself, though so many years ago it may be.

"So I started doing chores around his camp to pay him back." Caleb continued. "In the meantime I picked up quite a few skills from that old bastard."

"He sounds like quite the fellow." Abraham said. "What's he getting up to these days?"

Caleb's eyes flashed in pain at this question, he grew quiet for several moments before answering.

"He uh...Comanche." Caleb said softly with a pained swallow.

The other men only provided silence in response to this answer.

Squinting and wrinkling his nose to fight back a few tears, Caleb recounted the memory. "He saved me. Got wind of something bad one day." Caleb spoke distantly, his eyes looked upon the fire but his mind was back in the moment, reliving it all over again. "We had just sat down to supper one evening and then he jumped right to his feet. I had never seen him move so quick before that. He told me... "You run on boy. You run on and you don't look back."

Caleb stopped, clearing his throat for a moment. "He was a fine man." He spoke sadly. "A little rough around the edges but he was."

Abraham opened his mouth to reply but could find no words before Caleb started again.

"Well I listened, halfway anyway. I ran but I came back. Came back the next morning. They scalped him." Caleb choked out the last words like the bitter poison they were. "You don't hear about what happens to a scalped body." Caleb said, almost to himself. "When I found him... Maggots, ants, and all manner of bug were feasting on that raw flesh. Looked something like, wriggling hair from far away...and, and..."

Abraham placed a hand tightly on Caleb's shoulder, gripping it. "There weren't nothing you could have done Caleb."

"Let us not dwell on grisly things while food is hot." Buchanan interrupted coldly.

Abraham shot a look of fury at him for these words. A look of fury that Buchanan wholly ignored and continued to eat his food.

An hour passed as the men finished their food, packed up their belongings and set out once again. To the pain of Abraham, Caleb hadn't made a sound since his story. His eyes were distant, his head deep in painful thought.

Abraham stared now at Caleb's back as they walked, Buchanan leading another ten feet ahead. As they marched, Abraham searched his brain for something to ease the tension, to warm this cold atmosphere. Moments later, it came to him.

Quietly at first, and with no regard for melody or tune, Abraham began to sing.

"For we sent him out last night. To fetch some fish to fry. And he came back an hour later with a trout much bigger than I."

Buchanan and Caleb jumped a little and half-turned around, startled by the sudden noise. As he listened, Buchan grinned to himself at recognition of the old campfire song. After a moment, he cleared his throat and shrugged a little before joining in with the tune.

"The next night he went out hunting. To maybe kill a rabbit or two. Well he came back with a horse-load, and made a damn good stew."

Caleb grinned ear to ear as he walked, cheeks rosy and eyes upon the ground. He thought quietly, racking his brain for the next verse before it started. He remembered the words gradually. Trying his best not to laugh at the out of key and hoarse voices that sung around him, he joined in.

"And on the final morning, I said what have you got to brew? Well he poured me a cup of coffee, with some eggs and hog belly too!"

One can only imagine what the critters and bugs made of this 'cacophony of caterwauling' that had erupted in their home. But the joy and satisfaction that came through the men's voices would have caused anyone that was able, to join in.

Uproariously and brash, the men shouted the final verse together as a trio of tone-deafness.

"Praise to the cook. Hail to the cook. He's made something good tonight! And if the reaper comes tomorrow, well I can happily die!"

As the final line was sung, over and over again before the final stanza, the men burst into a roar of laughing and cheering. Some whistled or hollered in self congratulation at the fine musical number.

"Hail to the cook." Abraham said with a laugh as he slapped Caleb on the shoulder.

Gradually then, the laughter died down and sprang up again many times. But as is always the case, the good times will depart and leave the merry-makers silent. So too did the men finally quiet and resume their silent march.

"Bad omen." Buchanan spoke suddenly, bringing Abraham and Caleb to a stop behind him. He nodded to something ahead and Caleb and Abraham looked curiously for what it might be. At first they didn't see anything, but then it was clear.

There, pinned to a tree was a strange totem, a cluster of dried animal bones wrapped tightly with braided fur and hair. The totem hung at a crook in the tree and looked almost like a strange veil over the forest beyond, if one were to stand close enough that is.

"Injun land?" Abraham asked warily, looking to Buchanan.

Buchanan stared at the chime as the bones whistled faintly in the winter wind. "No." He said gruffly.

Abraham tilted his head and looked again at the thing. "How can you tell?" He asked inquisitively.

Buchanan raised a gloved hand and half-smiled as he pointed at the totem. "That. Means the land is cursed, or evil."

Buchanan walked closer to the whistling bones and knelt down to inspect them further. "Nah. This is the best thing we could have found. No self respecting redskin would be found inside this marker."

At this revelation, Abraham loosened the grip on his rifle. "How fortunate." He sighed out.

"All the same. I'd keep caution about. I ain't no expert, but I'm pretty damn sure." Buchanan said with a shrug. He stood then, dusting off the snow that clung to his trousers. "We'll be nearing Fort Preston then." He spoke confidently.

"How do you figure that?" Caleb spoke up.

Buchanan bobbed his head around to look at the boy, having almost forgotten he was there. "No better place to build an army fort than a wood with no savages." Buchanan walked ahead, signaling the others to follow. "That, and with as old as the quarrel of cats and dogs is, so too is the quarrel of the savage and the army."

As Abraham and Caleb passed the grisly marker and left it behind them, they couldn't help but take another look.

The bones and hair swung wistfully in the breeze, suredly nothing more than a trinket of foolish superstition. But, as they moved past it, the men almost felt like the totem watched them go, like the moon following a travelers gaze.

Silence once again enveloped the men as they continued on, silence that was unbroken until Caleb finally uttered the words that had been stewing in his mind.

"Abraham." Caleb said quietly.

"Yeah?" Abraham replied, not looking up.

"If I'm honest, those bones have got me a bit spooked." The boy said warily.

"I think all of us would be inclined to agree with that, Caleb." Abraham responded.

Caleb furrowed his brow and thought to himself some more before speaking again. "The Trapper used to tell me these stories. Real nasty stories about the injuns and their evil spirits."

"Oh?" Abraham offered out of politeness.

"Yeah." Caleb continued. "Real spooky stuff. He told me all about Witch Owls, Wendigos, uh... Skinwalkers..."

These strange names, more suitable for a tall tale than for casual conversation, provoked a half-laugh from Abraham. "And what might those things be?" He asked back.

"Well I don't entirely recall. Something about shapeshifting witch doctors, folk eating other folk." Caleb shrugged. "You know, good campfire talk."

Caleb grew silent a moment longer, something was swirling in his mind. "Anyhow, I sure am thinking about those tales now."

Abraham shook his head, producing a semi-genuine chuckle. "Well, best put it out of your thoughts. Ain't no sense worrying yourself over campfire tales and old bones."

Caleb nodded, more to himself than to Abraham. "Hey Abraham?" He asked again.

Abraham closed his eyes softly, growing slightly annoyed at the incessant chatter.

"Yes?" He asked again.

"I was thinking." Caleb continued. "Might be good of me to go catch some more game. Bring it to the fort as a peace offering of sorts."

Abraham nodded to himself. "You know? That ain't a bad idea." He said genuinely. "Well go on, but be careful and don't wander too far."

"You ain't gotta tell me twice." Caleb responded. He was already moving off the trail into the woods beyond. "I ain't too keen on exploring these woods more than I have to."

Buchanan spoke up from further ahead as he noticed Caleb crunching off into the trees.

"Where's the boy running off to?" He called back over his shoulder.

"Catch some game." Abraham said, while quickening his pace to bridge the gap between them.

Buchanan grinned in recollection of the hot meal that morning. Belly still full and content, he smiled.

"A fine idea." He said with a nod. "These poor Uncle Sam bastards are surely starved for something hot."

"I would imagine." Abraham spoke back.

Buchanan continued. "These past few months I've had some of the best eating I can recently recall. Well, up until this last week or two that is... The Army would do well to enlist some of the wives as cooks."

Abraham nodded absently, mostly ignoring the man who seemed to relish in the sound of his own voice.

"I suppose." He breathed out with a shrug. Only offering the bare minimum in reply at Buchanan's rambling tangent.

"You sure seem close to that boy Mr. Mercer. I seen you two since we set out." Buchanan said, half inquiring.

"It isn't quite by choice." Abraham replied. "He nearly latched onto me and Laura at journey's start. But, he has a good head on his shoulders. I look after him when I can."

Buchanan pressed on, leading the conversation in a direction Abraham wasn't entirely sure of.

"Your wife seemed quite fond of him too. Condolences of course." Buchanan continued, seemingly genuine.

A subtle anger flashed in Abraham's chest at the mention of his wife from the likes of this brute. But, he fought it back, attempting to keep the conversation civil.

"She did care for him." Abraham responded. "Laura saw him as a son I suppose. Always scolding him to wash, make sure he ate enough."

Abraham grew more quiet as his mind directed him to memories and flashes of his late wife. As he pictured her face, her smile, his heart grew somber at the recall.

"I did not know her well. But she seemed a good woman. I am sorry we lost her." Buchanan said, as authentically as someone like him could speak.

"Appreciated." Abraham replied, wiping his eyes hastily with his sleeve.

Taking a moment to regain his composure, Abraham spoke again. "I suppose with her now gone, I should be the one looking after him. What she would have wanted I'd imagine."

Whatever kindness Buchanan had previously offered, evaporated as a grin grew on his face with a quiet thought. "Now...I am not one to question virility lightly-" Buchanan started but was cut off.

Suddenly, out of the trees emerged three men, outlaws by the looks of them. Two of them stood at the front, guns ready and aimed at Buchanan and Abraham.

Their leader; Elliot Boothe, stood to the back of the gunman, a large swath of arrogance radiating from him.

Buchanan immediately went for his guns, a sight that Elliot frowned at, followed by the click of one of his henchmen's hammers.

"Slow down there mister." Elliot said with a snide grin. "Wouldn't want my friends to get jumpy."

Buchanan scowled back at the grinning man, violently gritting his teeth and contemplating silently. He looked the two armed henchmen up and down. One of them held a double barreled shotgun, both loads ready to unleash hell.

A moment later, Buchanan complied with an irritated grunt, relinquishing his hands to the sky.

"You there." Elliot commanded Abraham. "Drop that rifle."

Abraham shot a look at Buchanan who nodded slightly. Looking back to Elliot, he did as he was told and allowed the rifle to fall to the snow with a thud.

Elliot smiled and brought up his hands with mocking joy. "Now that we're all friends, we can start business."

"What do you want?" Abraham spat out angrily.

Abraham hadn't said anything funny, but Elliot's goons chuckled like he had.

"The toll mister." Elliot replied as if it were obvious.

"We don't have any money." Abraham shot back.

Elliot sighed and hung his head a little, his grin still everpresent. "Well that's quite a shame. Seeing as how you're on Bryant Boothe's territory." He exhaled. "And fellas, crossing said territory requires a toll."

Abraham spoke sideways to Buchanan, not taking his eyes off of Elliot. "Who the hell is Bryant Boothe?"

"He's a small-time cattle rustler and train robber." Buchanan offered back through gritted teeth. "By that information, I would gather this here is his brother; Elliot."

Elliot glared daggers at this simplified assessment of him and his kin.

"You show some goddamn respect!" One of the goons shouted, gun still pointed at Buchanan.

Elliot raised a hand, calling off the lackey. He then strode to Buchanan, nearly pressing his face into the old bounty hunter's.

"What's your name, friend?" Elliot asked Buchanan.

Mr. Buchanan almost audibly scoffed before responding. "You ain't my friend, and I ain't in the habit of giving my name to people who ain't."

Elliot smirked, nearly impressed by the grisled man's unfettered machismo. "You don't seem to understand your predicament, mister." Elliot said as he placed his hands on his hips.

"Oh I understand plenty." Buchanan spoke back. "You're a lily-livered peckerwood who compensates for his womanhood by acting big."

Elliot semi-smirked, doing his best to hide the scowl that rose up. And then, without warning, he struck Buchanan hard with the back of his hand.

As he took the hard blow that caused his hat to fall down into the snow, Buchanan simply turned his gaze back to meet Elliot's. Hiding his temper as well as he could, Buchanan looked at Elliot with an expression that seemed to say; "That all you've got?"

Amazed at the lack of effect his strike had provided, Elliot grinned. "Oh I'm going to enjoy killing you." He scoffed, doing his best to hide the fear that Buchanan's piercing eyes put into him.

As he stepped back and walked to join his goons, Elliot began to speak again. "Well. Seeing as how one of you has got a loud mouth and neither of you has got a red cent to your name. I suppose we're done here boys." He finished speaking with a shrug and moved to signal his men.

"Wait!" Abraham exclaimed.

What happened next, happened very quickly. It couldn't have been more than sixty seconds.

Though, the men in attendance at this shootout, would definitely attest to it being much longer than one mere minute, those that were left alive anyway.

Suddenly, Caleb burst from the trees, oblivious to the situation and the tense and deadly standoff.

In reflex, the sudden noise caused one of Elliot's men to turn and fire his pistol, the wild shot ripping into Caleb's side.

"No!" Abraham shouted, and rushed to the boy's aide. He sprinted across the clearing, giving no regard to the bullets that had begun to fly around him. He buried his face in Caleb's chest and pulled them both behind a tree for cover.

The man with the double barrel, startled by the shot, swung his body and pulled the trigger accidentally. Both barrels exploded and sent buckshot flying. The hot lead traveled upward, and over Elliot and the other man at his side. The buckshot zipped by terribly close, almost taking their heads off but ultimately missing.

Elliot fell to the ground, his ears ringing. The other man swung back around to engage Buchanan.

Buchanan drew his pistols; two black powder Colt Dragoons. He aimed at the revolver wielding man and fired. The lead ball ripped through the man's stomach, tearing through his intestines and taking several vertebrae off his spinal cord before bouncing sideways and staying put in the man's gut. The goon fell to the snow, knocked flat onto his back.

The man who had wildly fired the double barrel ran sideways and dove behind a thick tree, a shot fired by Buchanan narrowly missing him. Buchanan tried to turn his attention to Elliot, but a shot that whizzed by his head from behind the tree cover caused him to duck back himself.

Elliot, who had begun to pick himself off the snow, dashed to the gut-shot man and attempted to grab his dropped pistol. As he reached for the weapon, the mortally wounded man grabbed frantically at Elliot, shrieking in horrible pain.

"It burns! Oh God help me!" The man screamed, clutching his open-faced stomach.

Elliot fought against the hands that tried desperately to pull him closer. "Let go Goddammit!" Elliot yelled before ultimately deciding to fire a punch at the man's seeping belly. It had the desired effect. The man wailed horribly and let go of Elliot; who then decided to forfeit the shootout and make a run for it.

Locked into a firefight with the remaining man, Buchanan traded bullets from behind his cover.

Then, he heard it, though he shouldn't have. Such a small sound should have been easily missed over the chaos, but his ears were trained well. The metallic click of an empty gun spoke to him from over the commotion, and it told him it was time to end this foolishness.

Buchanan stood, walking forward to the tree and rounding it. The teary eyed face of a hysterical man, who had most definitely pissed his pants, greeted him.

"Please." The man said pitifully.

This was all he could get out before Buchanan stopped any other words that may have followed, with a bullet to the man's forehead.

Some motion in his peripherals caught Buchanan's attention and he looked up to see Elliot running in the distance, becoming smaller and smaller with every bounding leap. Buchanan raised his pistol, aiming steadily at the fleeing man.

He fired.

Despite the distance, the bullet nearly hit Elliot, but ultimately embedded itself into a tree next to him. The escaping coward disappeared into the forest a moment later, and Buchanan scowled.

"Goddammit." He huffed to himself.

Buchanan walked back toward Abraham and Caleb. As he passed the gut-shot man, whose desperate cries had diminished to pitiful whimpers, Buchanan ended his suffering without offering so much as a glance. He fired another bullet into the dying fellow who was finally silent.

Buchanan approached the cluster of legs and arms that was Abraham and Caleb. They were grouped together tightly, face-down in a snowbank behind a tree.

"You fellas dead?" Buchanan asked the pile.
Abraham rolled to his back and pulled Caleb up with him.

Buchanan stooped and gestured to Caleb's torso. "Let me see." He stated flatly.

Caleb grimaced and moaned as Abraham helped him lift up his shirt to see the wound.

"Turn him." Buchanan ordered calmly.

Abraham did as he was asked and turned Caleb as gently as he could, revealing a matching wound on his back. The bullet had passed through his side, just above his hip bone. While it is never ideal to be shot, in Caleb's case he was definitely fortunate. The bullet had passed through clean and had avoided any major organs.

Buchanan nodded, opened his pack, and began to rummage through it. He spoke without looking up. "Abraham. Any spare fabric you can find in your pack, tear it up. Long strips."

Abraham nodded distantly and jumped up to do as he was asked.

Producing a needle and thread, Buchanan inched closer to Caleb. "Appears to have passed through clean." He said as he unspooled thread and put it through the needle's eye.

"Am I to die Mr. Buchanan?" Caleb asked worriedly, his voice shaking with the flavor of pain.

Buchanan shook his head, not taking his eye off the needle as he worked. "I don't think so. So long as I can stitch it."

Buchanan leaned down and pulled the wound closed with his fingers. Slipping the needle into the torn flesh, he went to work.

Abraham tore up a final strip of fabric and presented a handful of them to Mr. Buchanan with a shaking hand.

Without really looking up much, Buchanan spoke. "Good. Hold 'em for a spell." Grabbing Caleb's shoulders into his hands, Buchanan pulled him forward. "Now the back. Lean forward, nice and easy."

Blood wept from the wound as Buchanan repeated his work again on Caleb's back. "Abraham." He spoke. "Tie those strips end to end. As best you can."

Following his muscles more than his mind, Abraham absent-mindedly nodded and did just that.

Using his teeth to bite the thread off, Buchanan finished the stitch. "Wrap him now Mr. Mercer. As tight as you can manage." Leaning back to let Abraham in, Buchanan wiped at his brow and watched as Caleb's wound was tautly wrapped with the scraps of fabric. Buchanan then stood, removing his coat.

"Here boy. Rest a moment." Buchanan said as he laid the coat on the ground next to Caleb.

As Caleb laid down with a grunt and a groan, Abraham stood, beginning to come out of his daze.

Buchanan, already several feet away, went to inspect the two dead men. He first rolled over the gut-shot fellow, a slushy pool of bloody snow, steaming as he did. He rifled through the man's pockets, but didn't find much.

Neither did anything useful come from the other dead man, upon Buchanan's inspection. He sighed and resigned himself to retrieving the corpses' weapons.

He once again approached Abraham and Caleb, a rifle stuffed under his arm and an extra pistol in his hand. "You know how to fire one of these, son?" Buchanan said to Caleb, his hand outstretched and holding the newly acquired gun.

Caleb nodded, looking to Abraham, and then back to Buchanan.

"Good." Buchanan replied and handed the weapon to Caleb. "Now if that peckerwood meanders back here, you dust him between the eyes. For me alright?"

Caleb grinned, as much as his condition would allow. "I'll dust him alright." He replied in a pained and hoarse whisper.

Buchanan smiled and slapped Caleb a little too hard on the cheek in support. He then stood and beckoned Abraham to follow.

Abraham, still running almost entirely on adrenaline, had finally begun to come to his senses. He followed Buchanan, but his head was elsewhere. His gaze was cast off, deep in thought. The past five minutes came rushing back to him all at once and his mind rapidly tried to catch up.

"Where are we going?" He finally asked Buchanan.

Buchanan heaved a leg up over a tall snowbank and continued deeper into the woods. "We're gonna have to pull him to the fort. Don't want those stitches to pop.

"You sure about giving him a gun? We're all pretty shook up. Him especially... he could get jumpy." Abraham said thoughtfully.

"It ain't loaded." Buchanan said with a huff as he walked to a tree and pulled at the bark. "But it'll make him feel better til we get back. Plus that Elliot piss-ant ain't coming back this way til he gets some more fellas with guns."

"I suppose that makes sense." Abraham replied.

It was then that Abraham noticed the peculiarity of what Buchanan was doing. The old gunfighter was dipping under logs and branches to get to the trunks of trees. He'd approach the base, tug at the bark, shake his head and move on.

"What are you doing exactly?" Abraham said with a raised brow.

"Husks of bark will make a fine sled. This time of year, some of the dead ones' bark will come clean off." Buchanan replied.

"That ain't bad." Abraham said, impressed. Then, he moved to help Buchanan's search.

Back on the trail, Caleb laid down on the coat Buchanan had left him on. The wetness of melting snow had begun to creep up the fabric and into his own clothes. He shivered, taking another look around in his limited point of view.

His side ached something awful, burning pain radiating from the stitching. He had tried to sit up, but remembering Buchanan's instructions, had resigned himself to staring at the dirty white sky.

The silence of the wilderness when one is alone is both awe-inspiring and claustrophobic. The quiet pushes in on one's eardrums, almost as if drawn in by the mind, searching anywhere for the call of familiar sound. But when that emptiness is suddenly penetrated, it mildly shocks the body.

However, when that silence is breached by a sound that should not be there, the accompanying shock is usually followed by the chill of apprehension. A sickening feeling of tightened muscles, sweeping gooseflesh, and shriveling testicles.

The hum of the surrounding silence was breached when a faint rustling sounded from down the trail.

Caleb heard it, but could not see. The sound had originated from past his feet, and he could only see just above the tips of his boots from where his head rested. He tried to roll to his side, but could only half-manage. Resting on his shoulder, he cast his gaze down the trail.

Nothing.

Nothing except the two freezing carcasses of the men that had shot him.

Caleb breathed a little bit easier, assuring himself that whatever sound he had heard was surely dreamt up by his mind. But, a sickening thought crossed Caleb's mind as he looked past the frozen corpses.

What if one of the bodies suddenly stirred?

He pushed the thought out of his mind as best he could, and tried to turn his thoughts elsewhere.

But then, something far worse, and something far more real than the reanimated corpses of gunned down outlaws appeared.

Suddenly, that something emerged from the trees.

Caleb's voice caught in his throat.

The cracking and snapping of another husk of bark coming off of a tree filled the woods around Buchanan and Abraham.

"Thank you Mr. Buchanan." Abraham said suddenly, breaking the silence.

"For?" Buchanan asked, not looking up from his work.

"Saving our lives. You sure were quick thinking back there."

"Thanks are not required." Buchanan said with a wave of his hand. "Just tell Clanton to pay me double when I get the brood to California."

Abraham laughed a little, still letting the remaining adrenaline depart from his veins. "I will do my best."

Screaming.

No, audible agony ripped through the forest then.

Both men felt the shock.

Tightened muscles. Sweeping Gooseflesh.

Shriveling Testicles.

Buchanan ran, not bothering to turn around and sprinted back toward the trail. "Get the bark."

Abraham and Buchanan burst from the trees, ready for anything, or so they thought. Hunched over behind Caleb, was an Indian, though unlike any that the men had ever seen. He was painted pale white, white as a ghost and nearly invisible with the snow surrounding him. His hair was dirty and matted, and his face stared out at them, emotionless as a stone golem.

Blood ran freely down Caleb's eyes and mouth as he thrashed this way and that.

His screams were the only sound, aside from the wet sawing and ripping of the Indian taking his scalp.

Buchanan fired first, more out of reflex than conscious thought. His shot missed, and the Indian bolted up and into the trees.

Abraham fired second, an animalistic and involuntary cry ripping from his mouth. Both the men's subsequent bullets did not find their target, and the Indian disappeared, much like the ghost he had materialized as.

Abraham slid next to Caleb, hands shaking and unsure of what to do. Buchanan ran past them, giving chase to the ghost. Moments later, with not a trace found of the attacker, he returned to the others.

Abraham sat in front of Caleb, his hands outstretched but not touching anything. Words formed on his lips but no sound came forth.

"More bandages Abraham!" Buchanan shouted as he took control.

Abraham lay still, shaking.

"I...don't....I...." Was all he could get out before Buchanan slapped him, hard.

"Do as I say!" He yelled.

Abraham jumped to his feet, and went to scrounge up whatever fabric he could find.

Buchanan assessed the damage, doing his best to hold Caleb steady.

While grisly and very bloody, the scalping had not been entirely successful. Caleb's scalp hung on to his skull still with a handful of sinewy connective tissue. The flopping, mangled flesh wiggled as Caleb shook back and forth in pain.

"My gun weren't loaded!" Caleb hissed out in a near whisper, his words heavy with excruciating agony.

Buchanan's gaze soured and he steadied his hands.

"This is gonna hurt like hell son." He warned the boy. And, as gingerly as he could, Buchanan took the flap of scalp in his hand and attempted to place the displaced tissue back into its rightful place.

This was more than Caleb could bear. With a final howl of torment, he fell silent, unconscious.

"Now Abraham!" Buchanan called.

Abraham had just finished tying a few more lengths of cloth together end to end. He sprinted back to Caleb and helped Buchanan wrap it from the top of the boy's head to under his jaw.

The front part of the scalp lifted up and away from the skull, pushed away by the force of the knot. Buchanan poked it back down and it fell into rest, like popping an air bubble on a pancake.

"We need to get to the fort. Now." Buchanan ordered.

Abraham rushed to the bark husks he had dropped, and brought them back over. Buchanan took them, laying down the coat Caleb had rested on, into the curvature of the bark. Taking a length of rope from his pack, he tied it around the makeshift sled.

"You said there were no injuns!" Abraham shouted suddenly and hysterically. "Couldn't be! Alright?! I mean... What the hell was that then?!"

Buchanan rolled Caleb onto the sled, not even looking up to acknowledge Abraham's outburst. "He's a rogue." He offered simply.

"What the hell does that mean?" Abraham demanded.

Buchanan stood and thrust the rope into Abraham's hands. "Means he don't belong to any tribe, don't observe any creed. He don't follow any rules. He's alone." Buchanan sniffed in sharply and expelled a wad of phlegm onto the snow. "Come on. Cold'll slow the bleeding well enough, but we need whiskey before any infection can set in."

Abraham looked down at the rope in his hands and began to pull the sled. The bark slid across the snow quite well. With a heavy and shaking breath, Abraham heaved again and moved to catch up to Buchanan who was already well ahead of them.

Chapter 4

An American flag bearing 37 stars whipped wildly in the wind atop Fort Preston. A blizzard was bearing down on the structure more and more by the minute.

Buchanan held a flaming torch that howled angrily in the cold gusts of wind. As he finally beheld the sight of the fort, he turned around and shouted over the wind at Abraham and Caleb behind him. Frost and snow clung to his eyebrows and hair as the cold stung his stubbled face.

"We've made it! Hurry it up!" Buchanan's hoarse voice shouted as it battled against the torrent of the forest wind.

Fort Preston itself was really only a fort in a technical sense; it was made of wood and had held soldiers. But, it was not an impressive structure. The log fence around the fort itself was only about 150 feet in length and about 100 in width. It was rectangular in shape and had but only one main gate, that swung on massive, rusty hinges.

Inside the splintering wood of the perimeter wall, the fort boasted three small cabins, a half-built watchtower, and a petite fire and kitchen area covered with a leaky awning.

At the far end was a soldiers barracks in an adirondack, (or three walled cabin) lean-to, decorated with three bunk bed cots on each wall.

At its capacity, the fort could hold only maybe thirty men. Its bleak and uninspiring appearance matched its purpose. Fort Preston was different from other army outposts, in that it was not for strategic placement of trained soldiers and tacticians, but for stowing away embarrassments and troublemakers. Men with enough weight to throw around, or connections, that they could not be hanged at the gallows, but *could be* stashed away in the cold reaches of the north-west, either until they died or their enlistment lapsed.

Buchanan squinted through the swirling snow as he crunched up to the wooden gate. Abraham moved as quickly as he could, not too far behind. Caleb lay on the sled behind him, motionless.

Buchanan pushed against the gate that creaked and moaned, but ultimately would not open. He lowered his torch and could see an iron chain stretched along both doors of the entrance. The chain went along both sides and then in through the slats in the beams, the lock obviously on the inside of the fort.

"Open up!" Buchanan shouted. "We've got wounded!"

No answer, no lights, and not so much as a sound from inside the hollow structure.

"Goddammit." Buchanan huffed, and pulled one of his pistols, firing two shots into the air. "Hello!?"

Abraham pulled Caleb to a stop just behind Buchanan. Frantically, he pulled the rope off from his shoulders and fell to the ground, vomiting and gasping for air.

Buchanan turned, mildly surprised at the sudden appearance of Abraham. The howling wind had masked any sound their approach might have made. Buchanan spun around, still squinting through the relentless white.

"Is he still with us Mr. Mercer?!" Buchanan shouted through the noise.

Abraham wiped his mouth of the sick and half-walked, half-crawled to Caleb's side. He dusted the collecting snow from the kid's face and body and placed his face just above Caleb's mouth and nose. A faint breath slightly warmed his frozen cheek and he looked back to Buchanan. "Only just!"

Buchanan nodded and raised his pistol again. This time, he aimed for a link in the iron chain.

He fired. His shaking, frozen hands caused the first shot to miss and splinter out the wood of the gate, as the slug embedded itself in the snow on the other side.

"Shit."

He steadied his hand and fired again. The lead ball collided with the iron of the chain and ripped through. Twisted shreds of hot metal were the only thing causing the chain not to fall from the gate and into the snow. A few bashes from the grip of Buchanan's pistol did the rest, and the chain gave way.

"Abraham! Help me!" Buchanan ordered.

Grunting and cursing the whole way, the men pulled at the two sides of the gate. Deep yawning and creaking bellowed from the wood, as they pulled the opening through the piling snow drifts.

At last, they had provided an entrance large enough for the men and the sled to squeeze through. Abraham retrieved Caleb and hauled him through the beckoning opening, with only blackness visible on the other side.

"Hello?!" Buchanan shouted, now inside of the fort. "We come in peace! We just need medicine!"

Behind him, Abraham had placed Caleb safely inside the fort and had grabbed both ends of the severed chain from outside, pulling them inward. Using his body weight this time instead of brute force, he pulled on the chain until the gate finally clambered shut.

Something caught Buchanan's eye on the gate and he walked toward it.

A rusty padlock jostled lazily on the chain that had secured the door. A lock that had rested inside the barrier of the fort.

If they were alone as they appeared to be, why would the lock be inside?

Stuck in a thought that was half remembered, he shook his head and went to help Abraham move the boy.

"Pick a cabin." Buchanan shouted ahead to the others. "We need to get him inside."

Abraham gave a half nod toward one of the small dwellings. The one that had been chosen was a small and nondescript log cabin. A large snowdrift was swept high up the front door, the white tendrils at the top of the snowbank reached nearly to the roof.

Beside the door, there was a small boarded up window and a hitching post adjacent to it.

Buchanan strode ahead in long, high steps. He reached the door and pawed at the drift that entombed the shack.

"Help me with this." Buchanan tossed at Abraham over his shoulder, through gasping breaths.

Abraham took a moment to assure that Caleb and the sled would not slide away down any small slope that may have been unnoticed, and then ran to Buchanan's side to help.

The wind grew louder, almost in a duet with the heavy gasps of the men as they dug.

Abraham threw a glance over to Caleb on the sled as he worked. He could only just see small and infrequent puffs of breath rising from the lips of the prone boy.

At last, when their trousers had soaked through and chilled their knees. When their fingers throbbed and ached, and with ripped and bleeding cuticles, they had finally unburied the door.

Abraham stood and went to retrieve Caleb. He reached him, and opted to carry the boy and leave the sled behind. With more strain than he had expected, he hoisted the young man up into his arms and lumbered back toward Buchanan.

After a couple of slams with his body weight against the door, the frozen seal on the wood broke free and the hinges creaked open. Retrieving his flame torch from the hole in the snow he had thrust it into, Buchanan tilted the flame toward the inside of the cabin.

Two small chairs were tucked underneath a circular wooden table on one end of the room. One large bed, with heavy quilts draped over it was pushed against the wall at the other end. In between the opposite sides of the oblong cabin, there were a few scattered chairs, crates, and a shelf against the wall that was opposite a small wood burning stove.

Buchanan turned and stepped aside, allowing Abraham to duck and enter with Caleb in his arms.

"Lay him down on the bed." Buchanan instructed.

With his boots clomping solidly along the uneven, wooden floor, he walked. Once, nearly tripping on a loose board, Abraham placed the wounded man on the bed as gently as he could.

Buchanan found some candles and lit them. He then threw the torch into the wood burning stove for the time being, and went rummaging through the crates and shelves. After a moment, he found a few mismatched bottles with varying colors and different amounts of liquid in them. He uncorked one and took a quick whiff.

He gagged.

"Piss." Buchanan spit out with disgust.

Recorking the bottle and returning it to the crate, he tried another.

This time, when he breathed in, his nose was not greeted with the scent of a very dehydrated soldier's urine, but the spiced burn of grain alcohol.

He stood, and walked to join Abraham and Caleb near the bed. "Abraham. The boy awake?" Buchanan asked gruffly.

"No, but still breathing." Abraham replied.

Buchanan gritted his teeth and swallowed. "Good. It's better this way." He cleared his throat and paused before he said his next words. "Peel back the scalp."

Abraham whipped his head around and looked at Buchanan, wide eyed. "What?" He croaked out, not consciously meaning to sound as hysteric as he did.

"Do as I say." Buchanan replied. "It'll have scabbed some, but it needs cleaned."

Abraham digested this idea for a moment before subtly nodding. He turned around and moved his hands slowly to the bandage. Crisp fabric stuck matted to Caleb's forehead and hair. Dried blood and frozen sweat made a sickening peeling sound as Abraham withdrew the rigid cloth.

Caleb stirred slightly at the discomfort, but ultimately remained unconscious.

As the last few inches of the bandage was unrolled from around the young man's head, Abraham could feel his mouth sweating and his stomach turning. With trembling hands, he reached for the puffed seam at the front of Caleb's scalp. An angry, blood crusted and reddened line ran around the length of the boy's forehead and disappeared into clusters of hair and gore.

Though he grimaced at the thought, Abraham couldn't put it out of his mind.

Long ago now, he had once been in Missouri.

He had wandered about in a general store while Laura had been negotiating prices of fabric. Bored and with time to kill, he had wandered to a small table of sweets.

He glanced over the horehound and licorice drops, peppermint sticks and more. Then, he spotted it. A ceramic jar. A jar that no doubt held sweet baked wafers and cookies, was on a shelf against the wall.

The jar itself had been molded to look like a bear, a smiling bear playing a marching drum. At the top of the jar, a dark seam ran around the length of the bear's forehead; the lid.

If one were to request one of the delectable sweets inside the smiling, musical bear, the clerk would pluck the top of the bear's head off and reach within to retrieve a wafer.

After bringing forth a sweet, the clerk would return the bear's scalp to its previous position with a clink of ceramic.

If only it were that easy.

Abraham shivered now at this memory as he reached toward the weeping seam atop the boy's scalp. His fingers found the wound, and reached within.

The lid atop Caleb's head did not lift up like a cookie jar, but peel, like the skin of a rabbit.

Whatever dreamland he had been roaming through moments before, Caleb was now present and conscious in this new, all too real hell. He shrieked with an unimaginable pain.

Buchanan stepped in with swiftness and poured the alcohol all over the open wound.

Caleb thrashed even more. Flying and clenched fists swung at the men that pinned him down in this endless torment. One of these balled fists struck Abraham in the groin, in the left testicle to be precise. He doubled over, but fought through the pain and pinned Caleb's shoulders to the bed.

Buchanan reached in with a rag that had been soaked in the spirits and wiped at the sinewy flesh and exposed bone. He brushed and scrubbed away the dirt and leaves that had found their way inside the opening, grinding his teeth as he did.

This was Caleb's breaking point, he went limp all at once. Once again, the boy was banished to unconsciousness.

Buchanan finished his work and carefully placed back the flopping scalp. He stood and wiped his hands. "Wrap him again. At least until we can find more clean bandages." He directed.

Abraham nodded and did as instructed with quaking hands.

"I need a breather." Buchanan huffed out and walked toward the chairs in the corner. Before Abraham could take his gaze from his bloody and trembling hands, Buchanan had collapsed into the chair with a crash.

Some time later, Buchanan now snored in a chair against the wall. Caleb had stabilized as much as circumstance would allow, and he now drifted in and out of sleep.

Once, the boy had awoken screaming and writhing and Abraham and Buchanan had had to pin him to the bed. Buchanan had forced him to drink the rest of the medicinal spirits and now the young man snored drunkenly.

Abraham sat at the small round table, his leather bound journal splayed out in front of him, a candle glowing at its side. He had already had a quill handy, but he had found the ink amongst the assortment of forgotten things in the cabin.

He had felt that sleep would not come, but he had tried anyway. A bedroll near his chair at the table was rolled out next to his feet. He had laid restlessly for nearly an hour and had decided to write in the meantime. After rummaging through his things, and at one point worried that he had lost it, he finally brought forth his journal.

It had been weeks since he had written in it. Too much pain and too much to be done.

But now, if he couldn't sleep, he thought he could at least document what had quickly developed into the most eventful period of his life.

An hour or two had passed, he wasn't sure. But he had finally caught up to the events of this very night. He dipped the quill into the ink again, and continued writing.

We have arrived at the fort. Caleb is in stable condition it seems, thanks to the help of Mr. Buchanan. Strangely, the fort seems all but abandoned. Though, we have decided to wait until morning to investigate further.

It has been some time since I have seen four walls and a roof from the inside. And yet, instead of comfort, this structure brings only to me subtle apprehension, for reasons that escape me.

We hope to find some provisions and supplies, And if possible, perhaps some indication of what happened to the men who once resided here.

My thoughts dwell on Laura. Her death has opened a void in my heart that I am nearly certain shall never be made whole. But part of me wonders if her death was a mercy from her God. I see no success from this journey and only a miserable end that we have seen fit to put off as long as possible, no matter the futility.

Nonetheless, I shall see this journey to the bitter end. I will do my best to care for the boy and toe the line with my colorful counterpart Mr. Buchanan.

While I am grateful for him, his vast well of knowledge, and experience. I do not trust him. I hope in time, I will be proven foolish.

-Abraham Chamberlain Mercer

Abraham wiped the quill and set it down. He blew lightly onto the wet ink to dry it and left the page open.

The fire had been stoked well in the past few hours, and the warmth of the coals made him feel safe as his eyelids grew heavier and heavier.

Chapter 5

Abraham stirred from his seat at the table. His neck ached something awful. His eyes were dryly stinging and he rubbed them with balled fists. Squinting in the darkness, he tried to make out the shapes of Buchanan and Caleb. The candles had long since burned out, and he now sat in total darkness, accompanied only by the howling of the shrieking wind outside.

"Buchanan?" Abraham groaned as he rubbed at his neck. He stood, stumbling over some unseen junk left on the floor.

As he reached the bed, he squinted in the blackness and realized with an ever growing horror, that the bed was empty. His eyes flicked quickly to the chair that Buchanan had slept in against the wall.

Empty.

His breath quickened and his heart pounded.

Suddenly, with a mighty, howling screech, the door to the cabin ripped open wildly, banging against the wall and battling its hinges with a crashing ferocity.

Abraham jumped back into the bed with a start. He stared at the open doorway and shivered at the bite of the cold.

Slowly, he stood, walking toward the opening, and out of it. The wind stung his eyes and froze his watery eyelashes. With several rounds of sticky blinking, he grimaced and tried to stare through the howling white.

The gate to the fort was ajar, the forest beyond seemingly examining him, like a rabbit in a wire cage.

"Hello?!" He called out into the torrential, freezing wind.

"Buchanan!" He shouted.

"Caleb!" He yelled.

And then, all at once, with a terrible suddenness, the gate to the fort slammed shut.

The wooden pires of the wall suddenly seemed to inch closer to him and when he turned, the cabin was gone. He was left totally alone in this rectangular prison of frozen and splintered wood.

The courtyard was empty, only barren and frozen soil within the confines of the walls. Closer and closer the walls moved in on him, and the air seemed to grow hot and hostile.

The jagged wood of the perimeter, now closely resembling razor sharp and angry teeth, pressed against him. More and more the unrelenting pressure of the walls pressed against his frame. He felt his shoulders go first, followed by his rib cage.

Abraham struggled to scream with the total absence of air in lungs. The squeeze that the fort held him in continued to grow more intense, until finally, his eyes burst from their sockets, like the cork of a champagne bottle.

"Abraham." A voice in the void spoke.

His eyes shot open then, his face pressed firmly against the pages of his journal.

Buchanan was standing at his side, his hand gripping his shoulder and shaking it.

Abraham blinked again, the fragmented pieces of the nightmare already fading away to the obscurity brought on by a new day. He sat up, the dried ink of the page he had finished writing in hours prior, peeled from his cheek as he did so.

"We need to find some food." Buchanan said.

Abraham nodded and brought himself to his feet, backward scrawlings had tattooed themselves to his drool encrusted cheek.

Buchanan noticed this and made the universal gesture one would make when another had something on their face.

Abraham nodded and licked his palm, smearing the ink until it blended into the brown and gray pattern of his long stubble.

"How is he?" Abraham inquired as his waking gaze fell upon Caleb.

"Well enough. Though it won't much matter if we all starve to death." Buchanan replied dryly.

Buchanan had walked to the front door and had begun battling against it, a newly piled drift just outside.

Finally, with a satisfying crunch, the door gave halfway and let a gleam of morning light in through the crack.

"Snow's let up." Buchanan remarked as he squeezed through the crack and yanked the door open further.

Abraham, still in the wobbly daze of sleep, followed him through the small slit of light in the door and shut it behind him.

Now, emerging from the cabin and seeing the fort in the light of the day for the first time, Abraham could fully see the unflinching bleakness of this place.

Frost clung to any surface devoid of snow. Creaking chains swung at the far side in the cooks quarters, hooks empty of any deer carcasses that may have once been drained there.

The nation's flag that he had only just seen in the glow of the falling snow the night before, was visible now in all of its muted and faded glory. Piss soaked ice and snow along the walls, shone through in spots that the drifts had somehow not covered.

The cold hand of total isolation gripped his aching shoulders and he took it all in. Accompanying this feeling was a bellowing grumble in his bowels. Alone in the most literal sense of the word.

"We'll start there." Buchanan spoke up, pulling Abraham from his daze.

He looked up and saw what Buchanan was pointing at; the largest cabin within the walls of the fort. No doubt the quarters of whoever the top brass may have been at one point, yet still just as bleak and unremarkable as the rest of the place.

Abraham agreed and followed Buchanan's cautious stride, keeping his feet low to the ground to avoid any slick spots that might cause him to fall.

After they had cleared the door of this new building, and finally gotten it to budge, they found themselves in a dingy and dusty "living room" of sorts.

Light filtered in through cracks in-between the logs. Lazy beams of sun were dancing on the fragments of dust and then vanishing.

The first thing Abraham spotted, was a large horse blanket folded neatly atop a wooden chest. He picked it up and shook out the rough wool, scrunching his nose against the ancient dust as he did so.

"This could make a lot of bandages." He remarked as he rolled the fabric back up.

"Grab it then." Buchanan replied without so much as turning. His eyes were on a cobweb covered lantern next to him. He picked it up, dusted it off, and after a moment or two, had it lit and glowing.

Then, something caught Abraham's eye. Atop the chest, where the blanket had been, was a journal. Not too dissimilar from his own with its leather bound covers. It lay there like a bug, discovered in hiding after overturning a rock.

"A journal." Abraham remarked to Buchanan as he picked it up and rifled through with a flicker of the pages.

Buchanan half-nodded, and offered a small grunt of acknowledgement. His attention was turned elsewhere, a petite set of cabinets fastened to the walls near another woodburning stove. He rummaged through the miscellaneous cupboard doors and drawers, tossing empty bottles and containers over his shoulder.

Finally, he withdrew a relatively small pouch, not much bigger than a tin of coffee. He unfurled the rope that fastened it closed and reached inside. When he withdrew his hand, a glaze of white powder clung to his fingers and palm. He tasted it. "Flour." Buchanan said. "Though I do quite despise hard tac."

Abraham, now done rifling through the journal, placed it into his breast pocket and looked again at the chest it had rested on. A basic padlock was fastened to the container, sealing it shut.

"Hmmm." Abraham breathed. "Might be something in there worth taking."

Buchanan turned and looked at the chest, noticed the lock and then retrieved a fire poker from the stove beside him. He walked to the chest, slid the slender, but tough metal into the gap in the latch and pressed his body weight down.

With a sharp squeal and a pop, the latch gave way and Buchanan half-stumbled, half-fell onto the ground. He dusted off his knees and pulled the chest open.

As one usually thinks when a container is locked and hidden away, it is expected that there must be something quite impressive inside.

Grandiose images of treasure, impressive valuables, or hidden correspondence will come to the mind. A marvelous bounty of gold coins, the loot of ten pirate kings spilling over the lips of the chest, seemingly never ending.

So too, did Abraham and Buchanan's heads dance with these glorious imaginings. As the lid cleared, Buchanan eagerly tilted his lantern to look inside.

The chest was nearly empty, save for a few canned goods and some dried meat. A bounty that even the most piss-poor sailor in all of Edward Teach's crew would not look twice at.

"For some reason I expected more." Abraham remarked. "Half expected a pile of gold coins."

"You fancy yourself a pirate?" Buchanan remarked with a half chuckle. "Nah. Looks like someone was simply not too intent on sharing."

"Buchanan." Abraham prodded as he helped gather the few meager supplies into his arms. "The state of this place. Just the layers of dust even... It's been long abandoned."

"I would be inclined to agree. Seems best to gather what we can, hunt and trap too. Then when we're ready, get back to the rest of the flock." Buchanan stood and groaned as he did; his knees upset at the way he had crouched. "Let's get going."

As they exited the second cabin and trunched across the frozen ground, they spotted something. A large cabinet, one that they had not seen before, was now visible from the direction they were walking.

"Buchanan. What do you make of that?" Abraham asked.

Buchanan looked up and dismissed the small, closet-like structure with little thought. "It's nothing."

"How can you tell?" Abraham threw back.

"Look at the size of it." Buchanan grunted. "I'd bet folding money it's a mess of shovels."

"Or guns." Abraham quipped.

Buchanan stopped and begrudgingly changed course toward the cabinet-closet. "Alright. You've got my attention." Buchanan stopped outside the door and placed the few things he carried onto the ground. He grabbed the iron handle of the closet and pulled.

"It's stuck." He said over his shoulder to Abraham.

"Maybe it's nailed shut." Abraham mused.

Buchanan grunted as he shifted more weight and pulled mightily against the stubborn door. "No... I've just about got... it..."

With a crack and a crunch, the door gave way, and something tumbled out and onto Buchanan. The weight of whatever it was, knocked him to the ground. With a huff of annoyed pain, he looked up at what must have been a sack of loose kindling.

It wasn't.

Buchanan suddenly found himself staring eye to eye with the gray voids of a frozen corpse. He shrieked with a nearly comical man-scream at the sudden fright of it. He heaved the emaciated and frozen bones off of himself and scrambled to his feet. His eyes shot to Abraham who was visibly fighting, but losing, the urge to burst out laughing at the chink in Buchanan's rough exterior.

"Not a Goddamn word." He hissed out at Abraham. He then looked down at the heap of bones and to the yawning open door of the cabinet. He looked to one and then to the other, then back again. Something clicked in his mind, though he wasn't immediately sure of what it was.

"And here I thought a man of your prowess and daring profession wouldn't recoil at the sight of a dead man." Abraham chided with a grin.

Buchanan didn't respond or even acknowledge the ribbing. Abraham furrowed a brow and looked to the body as Buchanan was.

"What is it?" He asked.

"He died in there." Buchanan stated coldly.

Abraham shrugged, no stranger to the company of death. "And?"

Buchanan gestured to a frozen puddle of brownish-gray liquid on the floor of the cabinet. "He shit and pissed himself until he died, and then some more after. That's what was sealing the door, frozen piss and liquid shit. It weren't locked. No. He hid in there of his own accord until he died."

Abraham, puzzled, looked to Buchanan again. "What does that mean?"

Buchanan shook his head. "I don't rightly know. Though I do not like any of the possibilities." He stooped, gathered his things and walked back toward the cabin. "Take him out somewhere. Far enough that scavengers won't be looming near us when he thaws."

Abraham breathed out with a huff. "Why me?"

"Because I believe I have interacted with him enough for one day. Do as I say." Buchanan said grumpily as he continued walking.

"Well at least take these things off my hands!" Abraham called up to Buchanan.

Buchanan stopped and turned. "Very well."

Abraham walked briskly up to him and transferred the few supplies he had carried into Buchanan's hands and turned back to the dirty work of the body.

"Wait." Buchanan stopped him. "Take this." He turned and tilted up his hip, the pistol in his holster reaching toward Abraham. "In case that rogue turns up again."

A cold chill of ice washed over Abraham's spine. He hadn't considered the near certainty that Caleb's butcher was still out there, lurking in the shadows and waiting to mutilate again.

"Thanks." Abraham said as he drew the pistol and tucked it into his belt. He tried his best to mask the quiver in his voice, but he knew he didn't do a very good job of it.

It was not the first time Abraham had buried a body, but this time was the easiest. Though the frozen man crackled and creaked with every step, and the smell was foul, he wasn't very heavy. He was already several hundred feet from the fort, walking back into the woods and he hadn't even broken a sweat.

He walked a while longer, looking for a sizable drift to toss the man into. The ground was frozen solid and though he didn't like it, a proper burial was out of the question.

A cluster of pines came into view ahead of him. A large snowdrift was piled up, and it sagged in between the two trees, not unlike a hammock. It would do for now.

Abraham dropped the man into the center of the drift, laying the corpse onto its back.

He hadn't noticed before, but the breast pocket of the man's coat had the name **CLIFFORD** stitched into it. He filed this away for later consideration and used his hands to pull snow over the man's legs and torso. He stopped before he had fully entombed the man, leaving his face uncovered and stood.

He stood there quietly for several moments of silent analysis. He looked into those frozen gray voids of the man's eyes, and thought.

Try as he had, he hadn't been able to close the eyelids. They were too frozen in place, both with the cold and in death. Now, those milky, sunken eyes stared at him, observing their own burial.

"Clifford." He thought to himself. He cleared his throat and furrowed his brow a little.

"Well Clifford." He spoke to the corpse. "It ain't much of a burial and I apologize. If there's something after this, I hope you're where you wanna be. Maybe on a porch swing on a hot day, with a jug of cold tea at your feet."

The corpse stared back blankly.

"Or…" Abraham changed course, he himself not unaware of the quite ludicrous nature of this moment. "Or at a saloon where the drinks never run dry. Cards out in front of you, always laying out a straight or a pair of aces."

The corpse stared back.

"Well. That's it then." Abraham crouched down and covered the man's face with the snow. He stood and began his walk back to the fort.

Now, if Abraham had stood and continued walking further into the woods, he might have turned at the forked tree and hopped over the small stream that ran trickling, under sheets of ice. Then, he might have walked up a small embankment and walked between two large boulders.

If he had, he would have tumbled downward into a pit of nearly thirty feet and fallen into a pile of bones. And, if he had laid there long enough, and trained his ears well enough, he would have heard something or some-things sleeping and chittering.

If he had.

Chapter 6

When he had returned to the fort and entered the open gate, he saw Buchanan sitting near a fire in the middle of the courtyard.

Atop the flames, a cast iron pan sizzled. Buchanan had melted some snow in a separate pan and mixed the steaming water with a few grips of flour. Using a wooden spoon, he mixed the sludgy liquid until it resembled a thick and depressing cake batter.

After sprinkling in some salt, he rolled the doughy mixture up into small cakes and set them onto the pan with a crackle. He glanced up at Abraham who had approached him, examining the cakes as they cooked.

"I came upon another chain and lock." Buchanan said as he flipped one of the hardtack biscuits over. "Best lock that gate behind you."

Abraham turned and looked around the ground, unable to spot the iron chain in the dimming glow of the evening light.

"Over there." Buchanan said with the point of a finger that was encrusted in flour.

Abraham spotted it. It was already wrapped through the gate and it lay draped across the entrance, he had probably stepped on it.

He walked to the chain, flinching a little at the freezing metal as he picked it up. Leaning back, he hauled the door closed with a loud creak.

Abraham raised an eyebrow to himself as the last slot of vision of the forest beyond, was hidden by the closing gate.

For a moment, but only a moment, he had thought he'd seen something looking at him from within the tangle of branches. When, a moment later he had shaken off the foolishness of this imagining and locked the gate, he turned back to Buchanan.

The man at the fire had stood and wrapped the hardtack into a square of fabric. After that, he wrapped his hand in another length of cloth and picked up a petite kettle from the fire that Abraham hadn't noticed before. Abraham's stomach groaned as he caught the faint smell of the cooking, even though he knew that what was to be served was quite sorry indeed.

Back in the cabin, with the stove roaring, Buchanan sat at the round table and nibbled at his share of the biscuits. He grimaced.

"Anytime I am forced to eat these, starvation gains a second glance from me." He remarked this to himself dryly, as he washed down the rough cake with a swig of the watery coffee.

Abraham didn't acknowledge Buchanan's critique of the food. He was at Caleb's side, trying his best to beckon the delirious man to eat.

At the smell of the food, Caleb had lost a few layers of his hazy trance and had opened glassy eyes to see. He had tried to speak but had only managed a tired groan. They had been dosing him with whatever spirits they could find for the pain, and quite regularly.

Though secretly, Buchanan did have a bottle or two squirreled away for his own consumption.

Thus far, Abraham had only been able to get Caleb to take tiny nibbles at the hardtack.

"Bites that were no doubt still floating around in his mouth." Abraham thought. He set down the biscuits and got Caleb to take a couple sips of the coffee before the man fell asleep once again. Abraham hung his head in defeat.

He composed himself a moment later and took to wiping the food from the corners of Caleb's mouth.

Buchanan, who had been holding a conversation with himself, spoke again. "Can't quite call this coffee neither. Barely found enough grounds for a single cup."

Abraham stood and joined the grumbling old man at the table. "Put him in a room with enough to complain about and you will never have silence." He thought to himself as he took his first bite of the tack. He coughed at the dryness of it and his hands flew out for something to drink, anything.

Buchanan laughed heartily and passed Abraham his own cup of coffee to have a swig and to wash down the sand he had just eaten.

"Give a fella hardtack in the desert and he'll die of strangulation before dehydration." Buchanan said with a laugh as Abraham tried his best to quell his coughing.

"I came upon a deck of cards." Buchanan continued. "Blackjack was always my game but I know a few others if you fancy a round."

After his hacking fit had finally subsided, Abraham opened his mouth to reply but was cut off.

BANG! BANG! BANG!

It was Buchanan's turn to choke on his food as both men jumped at the sound. Abraham picked up one of the rifles that leaned against the wall and walked to the door. Waiting there for a moment for Buchanan to collect himself and join him, he slowly opened the door.

With Buchanan behind him and his pistol drawn, Abraham crept out into the courtyard. They could see it now, but they had both been pretty sure of what was happening.

Across the courtyard from the cabin they had set up in, the gate was moving.

Moving, no. Slamming back and forth violently.

There was no wind, this early night was still. Someone or something was slamming itself into the gate over and over again.

Buchanan drew his pistol up and pulled the hammer back. Abraham saw this and pushed it up and away before Buchanan pulled the trigger.

"What the hell are you doing?" Abraham hissed at him.

"Dispatching whoever has come calling."

"It could be someone from the wagon party!" Abraham tried to reason with Buchanan.

Buchanan shook his head and pushed Abraham aside. "Nah." He raised his pistol again and aimed at the thrashing gate.

"Wait!" Abraham shouted. "I'll go look myself!"

Buchanan grunted, annoyed and shrugged. "Be my guest, Mr. Mercer." He lowered his pistol and gestured for Abraham to move.

Abraham nodded and began to walk slowly to the gate. He raised his rifle and aimed cautiously at the whipping chain and slamming gates, just on the off chance that he was wrong.

BANG! BANG! BANG!

And then, as abruptly as it had started, the gate halted its seizure and swayed lazily back with a creak.

Silence.

Abraham turned back to Buchanan with a quizzical expression. Buchanan offered little more than a shrug in reply. Abraham turned back to the gate and crept slowly up to it. When he had finally reached it, he shouldered his rifle and peered through the slats of the fence.

After several moments had passed and Abraham still peered through the peephole and into the woods beyond, Buchanan had grown impatient.

"Well?!" He hissed out across the courtyard.

Abraham stepped back from the fence and turned to Buchanan with a perplexed shrug. "Nothing. Absolutely nothing."

Wide eyed and with eyebrows cocked, Buchanan cleared his throat and holstered his pistol.

After some discussion and a few card games, the ominous and eerie feeling had dissipated into the warmth of the cabin.

Speculation had been discussed no doubt, but what they had ultimately settled on was the unsound verdict of "A freak gust of wind."

Buchanan now snored loudly on the bed next to Caleb. The bed was large enough to accommodate two men, but Abraham had cautioned the old man to lie still and give the boy plenty of room. This, of course, was met with a careless wave of Buchanan's hand before he collapsed into the bed next to the wounded man.

Abraham, not quite tired and still much more spooked than he was willing to admit, again had time to kill.

He had settled into his chair at the table and leaned it against the wall. He had brought forth a pipe and had scrounged some meager tobacco. After he had filled it, he patted his pockets for a match.

Something large and rectangular was in his breast pocket and for a moment he was confused as to what it was. He reached into his coat and brought out the mysterious object.

The journal he had found in the second cabin was now in his hand. He had completely forgotten about it.

He set it upon the table, finished his search for a match, lit his pipe and opened the mysterious book. He flipped through a few pages with mild interest, reading a few paragraphs here and there before landing on a page to read fully.

> *Colonel Mathers has not seemed himself since the*
> *savages led us into the bog.*
> *Many men have since fallen ill, bad blood from the insects*
> *within have taken them.*
> *Mathers seems quite intent on revenge and none of his*
> *advisors can disparage him. I myself do not see the point to*
> *goading or antagonizing these people any further.*
> *I can only quietly hope for peace.*
> *Peace that may carry until spring and that I may finally*
> *return home. I have still not seen Stephen's since the excursion.*
> *Most men have labeled him as a deserter, though I do not believe*
> *them.*

And as of late and as I write this, strange happenings around the fort make me worry that something nefarious has befallen him.

Abraham, now fully invested in this journal of an unknown soldier, turned the page quickly.

Stephen's has returned.
Always quite enjoying his company I rejoiced.
Yet, he does not seem himself. He has not spoken about the whereabouts of the other men that set out with him and he seems pale and sickly, yet very strong.
Something has changed in his eyes.
Though I have done my best to remain steadfast in my convictions of facts and reality, I cannot help but to feel something, something in my bones that there is a gravely wrong happening afoot.

Abraham flipped another page.

More men are missing. Others have inexplicably returned. Others, that have been gone so long that there is no conceivable reason that they should still be with us, and yet here they are, among the living.
All of those returned, seem to be shells of what they once were. But yet they seem stronger than the rest of us.

Hunger and fatigue has befallen me and many others but yet those that have returned seem able bodied.

Colonel Mathers has just informed me that the rations have finally run dry. He has instilled in me the seriousness of keeping mum. He advises panic will only make things worse, but I am of the belief that all the men are well aware of how terrible our predicament is.

Tomorrow a party of men will go out hunting.

I pray that they are successful.

Abraham flipped the page but frowned when the next one was empty. He flipped again and again til he found another page with more writing. The penmanship was strange and unlike the writings in the previous entries. The letters and words spiraled down the page queerly in unpredictable directions.

This is the end. This is the end. This is the end. The end the end the end.

Abraham squinted at the page and flipped it to the next. Finally, a legible entry.

Myself and Colonel Mathers are the only remaining
inhabitants left in this godforsaken fort.
The last thing we ate were our holsters and boots.
Boiling water did not soften them, but I gnawed at the
tanned hide and I imagined beef, warm savory beef dripping
with blood and fat.

Oh dear God and Creation.

I shall die here.

Abraham shivered as he read these last words. After a moment, and after long consideration, he flipped further. Mostly blank pages stared up at him and he felt that he had reached the end finally.

But then, he finally landed on a page with one angry, scrawling word printed on it.

HUNGER.

Then, a large and loud snore from Buchanan caused him to nearly shriek and fall from his seat. Moments later, when he had been able to reassure himself that he hadn't pissed his pants, he laughed cautiously. With a shake of his head he shut the book and tossed it back onto the table.

Hours later, Abraham awoke with a start. The outside of the cabin was still dark and black as pitch. And yet, the inside of the cabin was well lit, he could see everything.

He could see the horrifying fact that Buchanan and Caleb were gone.

Terror clutched Abraham's gut in an icy grasp as he bolted to his feet. The door was open behind him and his eyes darted back and forth around the room before he ultimately decided to run outside.

The gate was open and there were tracks. One set of boot prints and one set of drag marks adjacent the backwards and stumbling set of ghostly markers.

"Oh God. No." Abraham's mind told him.

He ran. At first he slipped and stumbled on the muddy slush but then found his footing. He jumped and jogged forward out of the gate, the gate that was terrifyingly wide open.

At once, he found himself outside. Cold was burning his throat and lungs as the fog of his breath shot outward like that of an angry bull.

He turned, and could see somehow and for some unknown reason, that the front of the fort now held a lake.

A vast, frozen and yawning lake that steamed upward in pockets of open water next to frozen clusters.

He screamed the names of his comrades but no sound could escape his lips.

He was alone, horribly and awfully alone. He tried again but could not form even the most basic building block of language; a grunt.

But then, across the ghostly and steaming surface of the new lake, he saw it.

Atop the icy surface, a rowboat cut. At the bow, a man.

Buchanan held a lantern that glowed with a phantom white. At his rear near the stern, Caleb sat quietly rowing. The raw flesh of his scalp glistened from the lantern and moonlight as he rowed heartily.

Again, Abraham shouted, but the cruel fate that had stolen his voice held firm.

A hand gripped his shoulder then, and shook him firmly. Pulling him from this godforsaken nightmare.

Chapter 7

Elliot Boothe awoke in his bedroll. It had been several days since he had run into camp, shamefully, like a whipped dog.

When awake, he hated the way that the attitude of the camp had shifted against him, mocking him.

So, whenever possible he would dwell as long as he could in the realm of sleep and dreams.

When he had run from those two assholes until his lungs burned, he had collapsed and slept for nearly another day under the fallen ears of a massive pine tree that had collapsed sometime prior.

When he awoke finally, his body ached and his head hurt; though his pride hurt worse.

He had made it back to camp that night, several hours later. And when he had stumbled back into the perimeter, the watchman had fetched his older brother at once.

"But what had that self-important, do-no-wrong bastard done?" Elliot thought angrily to himself.

Elliot had relayed the story of a simple shakedown robbery gone wrong, and how he had only just escaped with his life. After he'd told Bryant how the old man that was much more impressive than he looked, had gunned down his two compatriots and nearly himself. What had his dearly beloved brother said?

"Well now." Bryant Boothe had said. "It's a good thing you're back. It's just about your time to keep watch."

Bryant was embarrassed of his little brother, and regarded him poorly at every turn. Elliot knew that, and even still with that knowledge, he desperately sought Bryant's approval. A fact that he powerfully resented himself for.

Bryant had been made the unanimous leader of this outlaw party nearly seven years prior now. The day after this promotion, he had changed the name of the outfit from The Dan Crowder Gang to its now present glory, or rather; present shame, of The Bryant Boothe Gang.

Elliot missed Dan, and he missed the way his brother had been when he was still a lackey rather than the head honcho.

Now, staring up from his spot beneath the pine, the spot he had been demoted to after his disgrace, Elliot reminisced about how times back then had come to be; and how they had been.

He was back on the Boothe family ranch, just a few days after their drunk, asshole of a father had finally gone to meet the reaper.

Elliot remembered that fateful day that he and his brother had awoken to the thunderous sound of horses galloping; a lot of horses.

Bryant, only fourteen at the time, had clasped a hand over his brother's mouth and had offered the simple instruction of: "Shhhhh.."

Then, together, they had crept to the window and had seen the gang for the first time.

Dan Crowder; a bloody gunfighter, though not an unreasonable man had sat atop his horse and instructed his gang members that were now looting the Boothe family barn.

Bryant, Elliot remembered, had bolted to his feet and gotten his boots on before Elliot could pull his eyes away from the scene outside.

"You stay right there little brother." Bryant had said.

Elliot watched as his big brother had walked out to the kitchen from the small bedroom, and retrieved his father's rifle from its perch over the fireplace.

He remembered hearing Bryant kick open the door and fire a wild shot over the head of Dan Crowder and company.

But he didn't see what happened next.

Dusty Ellis; Dan Crowder's right-hand man at that time, but dead not too long after, had been waiting.

A moment after Bryant had kicked open the door and fired his wild shot, Dusty had tackled the young boy to the ground and struck his face savagely.

Elliot, upon hearing this commotion, ran to the door and had seen Dusty breaking his brother's nose with a fierce punch to the face.

"And then, what had the great and cowardly Elliot Boothe done then?" Elliot thought disgustedly to himself.

Elliot had slinked back into the shadows of the cabin and had cowered behind his father's old sitting chair.

Dan Crowder and company, now fully upon the house after the wild slug had zipped over their heads at the barn, had come to see what all the fuss was about.

Dan, seeing his partner Dusty now, as he was throttling the boy atop the porch, called him off.

Bryant had gasped for air and stumbled to his feet, small wiry fists raised, ready to continue the fight.

This show of foolish courage in the face of the jaded outlaw gang, had gotten Bryant a hearty laugh of both amusement and respect.

About an hour later, after Bryant had been subdued and Elliot had been coaxed out of his hiding spot in the house, they now sat in front of the outlaw king.

Mr. Crowder, who had taken it upon himself to make the sitting chair of the Boothe family patriarch, his temporary throne, looked upon the two boys who had been brought before him.

"You've got some balls on you yet boy." Dan had said to Bryant who was restrained at gunpoint on the floor next to Elliot.

"You're trespassing." Bryant's squeaky, fourteen year old voice had replied. "Judge Collins will have you hung."

This produced another laugh from the gang who had all found a spot to sit in the Boothe cabin.

"Oh will he?" Dan had replied with a blatant and slightly juvenile tone. "I should be plum scared then. Shouldn't I?"

"Damn right you should." Bryant shot out.

"I like this kid." One of the outlaws had said, though Elliot couldn't now recall who.

"Where's your Ma? Your Pa?" Dan had then inquired.

It was now Elliot's turn to speak. "I didn't ever know our Ma." The ten year old spoke, voice quivering. "Our Pa was a drunk, drank himself to death not three days ago."

"Hush your mouth!" Bryant had yelled to his brother. This had brought an overeager, backhanded smack from Dusty, a smack that caused him to be dismissed outside by Dan.

Bryant had fallen to his face from the blow and looked up at Dan, who was staring angrily at Dusty.

"Look kid." Dan had said as he'd reached into his coat. "We're taking all you've got here. You're welcome to tag along til we come across our next town. You're welcome to run right to the judge and tell 'em all that we've done." Dan had produced a pre-rolled cigarette from his coat, had lit it, and had passed it to the bleeding boy on the floor. "But, you've impressed me. And I think it would be a damn shame for you to do something that would make us have to put a bullet in your back."

Bryant's demeanor had begun to crack ever so slightly. He toked on the cigarette that the slick gunfighter had given him, coughing as he did.

Dan had then smiled one of those classic "Dan Crowder" grins that could make you feel like you'd be a fool to say no. "I think you boys should join up. We'll feed you, protect you, and teach you how to fight. I think you'll do much more than survive like you'd do here. You'd thrive and carve out a life for yourselves."

And that had been it. Nearly fifteen years now of living off the land. Robbing, killing and grifting their ways through life. And neither of them wishing for it to be any other way.

Seven years now that the consumption had finally gotten Dan. Seven years now that Bryant had gradually moved them more and more north from old Mexico as the bounty hunters and other interested parties had moved closer and closer in.

Elliot stood now, having lived long enough in this memory, and had pulled himself out of his slumber enough to stand.

He walked up the small hill that the den of the large pine had provided against the snow drift. He walked further up the hill toward the boss's tent.

To his brother's tent.

At his left, Maggie Henderson, wrung steaming water out of a shirt at the wash tub. He allowed a grin to form on his lips and offered a small wave. Maggie averted her eyes.

Elliot's chest burned with both embarrassment and jealousy.

"Stupid whore." He thought angrily to himself. "Wouldn't know the right man unless he paid in advance and blacked her eye. Stupid girl."

Maggie had joined them nearly three years ago now. She had been locked in the town jail after stabbing a man to death.

As gruesome as it sounds, Maggie had only killed the man after he had nearly strangled her, when there had been some confusion about what she would do with a payment of ten dollars.

That didn't matter to Elliot. All that mattered to him, was that she was a stupid whore that was a fool to spurn his advances. And it made him angrier every time it happened.

The day Maggie had joined, the gang had broken into the jail, had killed the weekend marshall and had broken out one of their members. A member that had gotten a little too drunk and had beaten a couple men within an inch of their lives.

Maggie had been there in the neighboring cell, and had talked her way into joining the outfit. She had proved her worth immensely since. She had a fair knowledge of medical care and other useful topics. She was well liked and a valuable member of their small community.

But to the sniveling and overcompensating example of nepotism, she was just a dumb whore.

Elliot had crested the hill now, where the boss's tent was erected at the top. He pushed through the two flaps and entered. Inside, he could see that at his brother's side were two men, his top men.

Hal Douglas; a grizzled and seasoned gunfighter who had been a trusted companion of Dan Crowder since the days of the gangs' infancy. Elliot didn't mind Hal too much. He was level headed and not prone to childish chiding or mocking. Though Elliot did not appreciate the pitiful look that was worn whenever Hal looked at him.

At his left, opposite Hal was Delbert McKinley. Delbert, who according to Elliot was little more than a worm in his brother's ear. He hated Delbert and his stupid wiry face that scowled behind high cheekbones. Delbert didn't like Elliot back, and that was fine with the both of them.

There was a hushed conversation going on between the three men, one that got noticeably quieter when Elliot had entered.

"Bryant." Elliot interjected into the hushed mumbling.

Bryant and the others looked up, visibly annoyed at the interruption.

"What is it?"

"What're we gonna do?" Elliot asked excitedly.

Bryant furrowed a brow, signaling to Elliot that he had no clue what in the fresh hell he was talking about.

"About those men?" Elliot continued. "They're laying low at old Fort Preston. I know they are!"

Bryant managed a patronizing grin at this, but no more. "The two old men and a boy that whooped ya? Sent ya hauling ass back here with your tail between your legs?" Bryant chuckled. "What the hell for?"

Elliot, who admittedly was blowing up a "lead" more than it was worth, needed something to be brought back into the good graces of his brother. "It's a lead. Could be something there."

"What?" Bryant looked up fully now, growing visibly irritated. "What lead? Two old men without a penny to their names and a gutshot boy?"

"They ain't alone." Elliot offered insistently. "I got the sense they were a scouting party. Me and that new kid, Miller, we trudged back the way they came. We found a whole handcart company."

"Oh?" Bryant asked. "They didn't by chance have a man of the cloth walking 'round did they? A Preacher?"

"They did!" Elliot shot back, exceedingly pleased.

Bryant laughed and shook his head. "You've got a lot to learn, little brother. Religious pilgrims ain't got a pot to piss in, let alone any wealth to share. They've given it all to God. Sold it all to make their journey." Bryant shook his head and looked closely at Elliot. "You're grasping at straws after you got caught with your pants down. Take your lumps like a Goddamn man, and let it go." Bryant gave Elliot a dismissive look and turned back to the discussion at hand with his men.

Elliot could feel his face burning up and growing crimson at every word. His head fumed and he wanted nothing more than to jump across the table and wallop his prideful brother. He stared angrily at Bryant and the two lackey's at his side, he had no words and that infuriated him.

After some time, Bryant looked up again at Elliot. "Is that all? You've got to clean up the stables today if I'm not mistaken. Go on now. Daylight's burning."

This pushed Elliot over the edge. He wanted to curse and shout, to blacken Delbert's eyes and to spit in his brother's face. But he did none of those things. He only managed a choked and irritated gurgle and stormed from the tent with a huff.

Elliot stomped back down the hill to his pitiful quarters. When he got back, he saw Miller Pataky; the newest greenhorn of the gang, waiting for him, standing next to his bedroll.

"What do you want?" Elliot hissed at the kid.

Miller played with his hands idly for a moment before finding his words. "I went back to that camp. The one with them handcart pioneers." The boy sheepishly said.

Elliot raised an eyebrow, he was now all ears. "And?"

"That Preacher, the one we seen walking all over that camp. I snuck down and got into his tent. He's got a big old safe in that thing." Miller said.

Elliot grinned but quickly wiped it away before Miller could see. "Does he now?" Elliot sighed happily.

"God's truth." Miller replied. "It's too big to get out of there ourselves, and ain't no wagon getting in or outta there til the snow melts."

Elliot put his hand on the boy's shoulder and let him continue.

"But I ain't seen more than three rifles to that whole caravan. We could take em. Me and you, just ourselves, easy. Smack that old preacher up something awful til he cracks it open for us." Miller finished laying out his idea with his consistently timid tone.

"It's good." Elliot remarked. "How come you ain't told the boss about this?"

Miller shrugged. "I thought it might be a good one to surprise him with. Get me into some better graces. Better than the shit work he's always got me running anyway." Miller raised a hand suddenly as an idea formed in his head and his mouth tried to catch up. "I know he's your brother and I ain't trying no mutiny. I seen the way you look when he's around. You don't like him neither. But he's the boss and we gotta make him happy if'n we want anything better for ourselves."

Elliot raised a hand. "I understand you Miller. I understand you clear as day. We'll leave here right soon. Best to get a jump on it."

Miller grinned as Elliot patted him on the back and moved to his pack to begin gathering his things.

Chapter 8

The past couple days at the fort had moved by without incident. Buchanan and Abraham had tried to hunt, but had yet to come up with anything besides the odd squirrel. The odd squirrel that was not much of anything when divided up between three men. Well, two men and one very sick boy.

Abraham had remained hopeful with Caleb's recovery and had been somewhat rewarded. The boy had begun to stay awake for longer intervals and had even managed some very limited conversation.

But now, Abraham stood outside the fort, in the act of emptying Caleb's bedpan. Regrettably, he could see that the deposit in the old coffee tin was a dark, brownish color, and it reeked of dehydration.

They needed food, but more importantly he needed Caleb to eat it. He needed to eat and drink well, much more than any of them had been if he was ever going to recover. They needed meat, needed broth.

And then, as he turned to greet the footsteps that had sounded behind him, it would seem as if Buchanan had read his mind.

"Come on." Buchanan said authoritatively and slung a rifle into Abraham's hands.

"Where are we going?" Abraham asked, though he felt he already knew the answer.

"Hunting." Buchanan responded. "For Goddamn anything."

And so it had begun. The grand hunting trip for; anything. Abraham had followed Buchanan out of the gate and they now ventured into the forest and beyond.

They walked now, and *had* walked for what seemed like at least a couple hours. A couple of piss-poor trackers and guides, hunting the meat of only God-knew-what.

Abraham, not having had the best ration of sleep in the past several sets of nights, lulled in and out of attentiveness.

He himself was honestly unsure of where the hell he was going in this condemned venture and in that moment of unsureness, he was allowed to drift in his thoughts.

Usually, these moments he appreciated. Moments where he could perform a quiet and introspective inventory. However, in this instance, cynicism and impotent irritation, wrought on by the lack of sleep and food pushed in.

"What sort of beast are we tracking Mr. Buchanan?" He whined, physically wincing at his irritating tone as he spoke.

"Whatever may be foolish enough to cross the sights of our rifles." Buchanan had replied, his unrelenting, and exhausting tone of a man's man, shining through and true.

Abraham really disliked Buchanan at times. Or maybe he didn't mind the old man, he wasn't sure. His head was a misty forest that he struggled to navigate through.

"You know." Abraham breathed, hating himself as he said it. "I would be grateful to partake in horse, if we had it."

Buchanan gave his usual gruff grunt of acknowledgement, trying to quell this tangent of discussion before it developed. But still, Abraham persisted.

"My Mama, a thousand years ago it feels like. Well, she would surely be cooking a fine roast of beef." Abraham breathed in loudly. Suddenly, he was quite sure he could almost smell the fictional food.

He continued, his mouth salivating as he built the pictures in his mind. "Fat crackling in the pot... Even more certain, there would be biscuits baked upon the coals." Abraham sighed again, imagining the buttery and flaky, but sadly, imaginary baked goods.

"Goddamn biscuits that you could pull apart with the slightest twist of the wrist."

"Stop!" Buchanan nearly shouted.

Abraham jumped, his daydream shattered by the solid rock that Buchanan had hurled into his distant fancy. Buchanan's hand was suddenly squeezing his shoulder very hard.

"Enough." Buchanan said surely. "What you are doing is enough to drive a man mad."

Abraham rolled his eyes in reflex and embarrassment. He scowled at him, and at the bear paw that had locked onto his shoulder like a metal vice. But ultimately, he knew how right Buchanan was.

"Mad!" Buchanan huffed seriously. "Do you hear me, Mister Mercer? I know very well with what you are grappling. But you quell it, you quell it now. Or you'll drive us all mad."

Abraham shook his head and battled pride a moment longer before responding. "Of course, Mr. Buchanan. No point in torturing ourselves. I do apologize."

Buchanan, sometimes the living embodiment of a grumpy-old-man, huffed to himself and continued walking, eyeing the trees for game.

Game.

Yes, Game, that distant and hopeful thought that had brought them out into this wilderness in the first place. But none of the inhabitants of this wood had revealed themselves yet. Not even the odd squirrel had come out to say hello like he sometimes would.

For a while longer, they continued. Silence mostly held between them, aside from the moment here or there, where one of them thought they had spotted something.

Silence was to be expected. After all, they didn't really have much in common, not much common ground to stand together on. Buchanan seemed to hold a quiet respect for Abraham, and Abraham held the same back. But apart from that, there wasn't much to say between them in the sense of "small talk".

And so they would continue, a marriage of necessity. An undecided and unwanted marriage that Clanton had forced them into, in what now seemed like a certifiable eternity ago.

And then, Buchanan spoke. He had been deliberating quietly on what he might float out to break the silence. But as one would expect, the topic he chose was grim and something only Buchanan would believe

could be held in the institution of "polite conversation."
And like Buchanan himself, this topic held more than one
would see at face value.

"When I was just a boy, no more than eleven..."
Buchanan began, striking Abraham with a bit of surprise at
the break in silence. "My mother begat a baby brother. I
had had a younger brother before that, but he had been
taken young, a year or so prior."

Abraham raised his eyebrows and tuned in
attentively. Anyone would be interested in this glimpse
beyond the impenetrable armor that supposedly held a
being known as Buchanan underneath.

"Then, one year the famine hit." Suddenly,
Buchanan was distant, transported back in time to the
actual instance of existence that this memory had occurred
in.

"I remember I gnawed on a deer blanket until it
was full of holes. I remember my Mama crying because she
could not suckle my baby brother." Buchanan cleared his
throat, distracting from the fact that tears had requested to
vacate from his eyes.

"Starvation." Buchanan coughed. "Starvation plain
and simple was what it was. I have known true hunger Mr.
Mercer. I know the beast all too well."

Abraham, now pulled from his shamefully juvenile complaints and daydreams, listened intently with what the old gunfighter had to say.

"Hungry, so Goddamn hungry... My baby brother would wail, would howl. All of our heads ached from the hunger. My Ma's, My Pa's, My own Goddamn head."

Buchanan was very far away now. He was dwelling in something he had not dredged up from the swampy waters of his subconscious in a long time. "Baby brother could not be consoled. No one could help him. He was wilting away by the hour." Buchanan sniffed a little.

Abraham furrowed and squinted his eyes. This tale had not been something he had expected. For so long now, Buchanan had not been a human, but rather a sentry crafted in some assembly line, made from conception to serve his purpose. But nonetheless, the old man continued the baring of his heart.

"So. As not to prolong the child's suffering... My Pa..." Buchanan choked for a moment. "He snuffed him out with a rag."

The brutal honesty of this moment wringed forth from Abraham a single word.

"Christ."

"He thought no one had seen." Buchanan said absent mindedly. "But I seen. I saw what he done."

"I'm sorry." Abraham offered, still shocked at the bluntness of the tale.

Buchanan cleared his throat and receded back into his usual and comfortable shell. "Not a sorry thing. He did what he needed to. Took away another mouth that would not make it through. Another mouth that would slow or kill those that were stronger."

Abraham stopped fully now and was reeled into his mind. Something in his head was telling him there was something he was missing. Like when someone tells a joke that's gone over your head and all around you everyone laughs. But moments later, a horrible realization clicked into place and transformed ideas into thoughts, and thoughts into words.

"You're not talking about Caleb." Abraham said blankly, not wanting to believe.

Buchanan looked at him coldly. "He will die. That is near certain."

"You don't know that!" Abraham shouted back. His hands were now very aware of the grip they held on his rifle.

"Lower your voice Goddammit!" Buchanan hissed as he moved close to Abraham. "He's no use to us. The boy hasn't uttered more than four words in days. You cling to him and you'll kill us all."

Abraham shook his head. "He's recovering. He'll pull through."

"You think I want to stay here? At this fort? These discarded bones filled with nothing but empty cupboards and ghosts?" Buchanan retorted. "We're tied to a lead weight with a rising tide."

Abraham opened his mouth to say something again but suddenly a sharp and shrill whistle from down the trail silenced him.

"Drop 'em!" A voice that came from an unseen body instructed.

Still stunned with surprise, Abraham and Buchanan darted their eyes from tree to tree.

"Do as I say Goddammit!" The voice yelled again.

Buchanan scowled vaguely in the direction of the instructions and dropped his guns. But as his last pistol left his hand, he thought to himself that he knew that voice.

"You got a deathwish mister?!" The voice shouted again.

Buchanan started to open his mouth to point out that he had in fact, "dropped em" when he noticed that he wasn't the one being shouted at.

Abraham still held his rifle tightly and defiantly, an expression on his face of pure aggression.

Buchanan stared more in shock at this face, a face he had never seen before, rather than the unseen attacker in the woods. Abraham looked different, looked fierce, and it was Goddamn unsettling.

"Drop it Abraham. It's alright." Buchanan said cautiously.

He spoke carefully, thinking that if he caused enough offense unintentionally, that the rifle would be used on him first.

Abraham looked slowly to Buchanan and then did, in fact, drop it.

Out of the trees then, Elliot Boothe emerged, only twenty or thirty feet from the men. He had a rifle of his own and it was pointed at them.

"No, not a rifle." Buchanan thought. "A double barrel, and at this range a quick flex of his trigger finger would mulch us both."

"What the hell do you want?" Abraham shot coldly.

Buchanan winced. The last thing someone should do when they've cornered a cowardly rat, is to jab it further. Buchanan was brave, but he wasn't fuckin' stupid.

Elliot grinned. "That wagon train up the ways a piece? That where y'all come from?"

Abraham's face dropped another shade into the blind rage of a man that has been pushed too far. "How do you know that?" He hissed at the gun toting chicken-shit.

"They're gone. All dead." Elliot said with a smirk laced with fiery acid. "All shot to swiss cheese."

"Bullshit." Buchanan spat back, his hands still raised heavenward.

Elliot's smile grew more, though that seemed impossible, even in theory. "God's truth. That old preacher? He was my favorite. He sure could holler loud."

Abraham suddenly and inexplicably began to walk forward. Slowly at first, but then more deliberate and bigger steps.

Of course Elliot had immediately protested, his trigger finger visibly itchy. "Get back! Don't you move Goddammit!"

Abraham didn't even give this command a moment's consideration. He moved ever closer to the business end of the double barrel, unhindered.

"Abraham!" Buchanan hissed behind him, attempting to call his seemingly suicidal comrade back.

Elliot seemed to have suddenly developed debilitating tremors. His hands shook and grew more wild by each crunching step of Abraham. "I'll shoot you mister! Don't you test me!"

"He's alone." Abraham said definitively.

"Get back Goddamn you!" Elliot cried.

Buchanan grinned, both in pride and shock. He bent down to pick up his guns slowly, much to the discomfort of Elliot.

Out of the trees suddenly, another man bolted, running back up the trail. Buchanan, startled by this, fired blindly at the running blur, he missed.

The crack of the gunshot had snapped the last of Elliot's nerve, he dropped the shotgun to the snow and raised his hands. "Miller!" He cried over his shoulder at the fleeing boy. "You filthy coward!"

Abraham had come upon Elliot now, the shuddering assailant looked into Mr. Mercer's face and uttered a single word.

"Wait."

Abraham didn't. He punched Elliot across the jaw as hard as he could. The Boothe boy fell flat on his back from the force of the strike. Before he could utter another word, Abraham was upon him. His blows rained upon Elliot one after the other. Abraham grabbed a fistful of the kid's shirt and brought hell down upon his face.

Everything came out with each progressing strike. The hate and hurt at losing everything he had left in this world, and everything he had been reduced to. He did not hold back and rearranged the face of this sniveling coward as savagely as he could.

The crunches and squelches of the blows caused even Buchanan to flinch slightly, though he did not try to stop Abraham.

At last, with bloody and swelling knuckles, Abraham had exhausted himself, though he hadn't extinguished his rage. He stood and grabbed the dropped

double barrel, opened it, checked the shells and closed it
again.

Elliot, though mostly blinded from swelling and
blood that had leaked into his eyes, knew the sound of the
weapon.

"Please mister." Elliot gurgled out through his
bloody hole of a mouth. A mouth that continuously filled
and choked his words, both with fluid and with the odd
tooth.

Abraham raised the gun, standing over the bleeding
man.

Buchanan didn't say a word, it didn't matter what
he thought of this development, he had been here before
and knew it was not his business to interrupt. Hot and
furious retribution was taking place before him and he
would let it play out as it would.

Abraham pulled back both the hammers,
something that Elliot hadn't even done.

First, he aimed at the Boothe boy's head.

The pitifully weeping man could see this, though
not very well. He whimpered and pleaded with
outstretched hands. He wailed and moaned through words
that were clustered with sobs.

The head wasn't good enough. Abraham wanted to quench every base desire for blood, for retribution. He wanted to regress into the lowest form of carnal human his instincts knew, and to relish in every bit of the brutality.

Part of him though, at least, a part now buried under the raging current of hate, begged him not to.

He lowered the gun at the Boothe boy's belly. It was likely to be just as immediately fatal, but not as much as the head. If both of these barrels filled with buckshot somehow managed not to bifurcate this groveling, piss soaked coward, he would justly suffer moments longer.

He squeezed both of the triggers.

An absolute massacre. A description that should always seem apt to describe the carnage two point blank shotgun blasts would produce. The parts and pieces that normally assemble a human being, and all of their inner workings are instantly mulched.

Stomach, lungs, liver, pancreas, intestines; all just names of past lives for the now indistinguishable, steaming and wet mass of mulched meat. The force of the blast will rip inward first, and then launch back outward in the direction of the individual who has decided to liquify another person.

So too, did a very similar outcome happen on this wet and bleak day to Abraham Mercer and his unfortunate victim, Elliot Boothe.

Blood, guts and sinew catapulted upward directly into Abraham's face and showered back down over him. Buchanan had stepped aside, knowing full well what was coming.

It hit him with a warmth at first, a warmth he was grateful for, given the bitter cold of the day. A gratefulness that quickly subsided, both at the realization of what he had just done, and at the sickening taste of iron that had shot into his mouth and nose.

He stared down as his eyes cleared and he took in the grisly sight. For a moment he hated himself, hated that he could perform such a brutal, and cold act that was so unlike what he believed himself to be; a decent man.

But a moment later, that guilt washed away in the remembrance of the Boothe boy's claims. He had done what he had for Clanton, for Laura, for Caleb if he didn't recover and for every other poor soul this bushwacking bastard had killed in his too many years of life.

Despite this justification within himself, the adrenaline had begun to wear off and his knees buckled. Without even thinking he would, he vomited suddenly. The meager contents of his stomach mixed with the leaking mixture of the Boothe boy and made him wretch again.

When his empty stomach could wring out no more blood from the turnip, he sat on his hands and knees gasping for air.

Then, Buchanan's hand was on his shoulder. "You alright?"

He was not. But, nonetheless he nodded.

Several moments passed of lonely wind having a conversation with itself before Buchanan spoke again. "How'd you figure he was alone?"

"I didn't." Abraham gasped out. "Not til I started walking. Wrong guess anyway, not that it mattered." He looked at the blood that covered every inch of his hands and arms. "You think he was telling the truth? You think they're really dead?"

Buchanan was quiet for a moment as he considered this. "His brother would certainly have enough men for such a thing. Ain't too hard to take a caravan full of exhausted men and sick women and children. Cowardly."

"Why'd he come without him then?" Abraham wondered aloud. His eyes had begun to sprout tears and he fought them back, though he didn't think he could hold them long.

"Hard to say. Maybe he wasn't supposed to. Maybe he wanted to rub salt in the wound of a personal vendetta. I doubt Bryant would care whether we knew or not." Buchanan replied. "Clanton did have the key to Jacobs' safe. There was a lot of Goddamn money in there. Plenty of reason." He sighed and put a hand under Abraham's shoulder to pull him up from his knees. "Either way. I think I believe him, as unfortunate as that may be."

Abraham stifled a sob. "What do we do now? Where does that leave us?" He asked through a croak.

"Same as we've been doing." Buchanan replied. "Trying to survive. We'll have to hope we can ride out the rest of the winter in the fort, trudge on when the snow melts."

Abraham was quiet. There was too much to think on, too much to process. He nodded a little bit, but that was all.

"I reckon, we head back. Don't think there'll be much game hanging around after all that commotion." Buchanan said and began to walk, beckoning Abraham to follow. He turned and stopped suddenly. "We best sleep light for the next while. Lest there be retribution for what you've done here. There almost certainly will be."

And so they had ventured back to the fort, which luckily still lay undisturbed in its natural perch at the edge of the forest. Caleb lay sleeping in the bed when they entered the cabin and Buchanan had wasted no time in joining him.

Now, he snored loudly next to the boy whose breaths, for the first time since the attack had begun to not sound quite as ragged.

Abraham maintained his recently chosen, regular position at the table and wrote somberly in his journal.

With the loss of our comrades I am left unsure of what direction to continue. Do I attempt to venture somehow onward and leave Caleb at the hands of this mercenary? Do I attempt to return to the wagon train even though only death may greet me?

Food is wearing thin.

I try to feed and water Caleb though.
While his intake is still pitiful, tonight was an
improvement. He may pull through after all.
But, will that be a mercy? Or will it be a cruelty?
Nothing more than a prolonged death?

There is too much to think on, and too much to put at
the back of the mind.

I hope that if Clanton is still somehow... alive, that he
prays just as feverishly as he always has.

We will need every bit of God's grace in the coming days.

Chapter 9

Miller Pataky ran blindly in what he hoped was the direction of camp. Elliot was dead now, he knew that certainly.

He had lost direction of where he and Elliot had tied the horses, and now he wandered in a panic through the encroaching dark.

"A foolish idea." He thought now. "A foolish Goddamn idea to come out, only to antagonize those two."

Those two batshit crazy men that he was sure he could hear with every snap of a twig or strange animal call the night offered.

They were pursuing him and gaining ground, he was certain.

They weren't.

He ducked under a felled pine limb that he thought looked horribly familiar from earlier in his meandering quest through the dark.

He jumped over a boulder and took a few more steps. But then, as if by some horrible trick, the ground beneath his feet seemed to vanish from existence.

He fell, plunging down into darkness. He rolled head over heels, crashing into sticks and rocks.

His leg was thrust into a gap between a root and he felt bones snap as he twisted over it awkwardly. Blinding pain shot up like fire from his leg as he rolled a moment longer, and then slid to a stop.

Shock kept his leg dull for a few moments as he tried to understand where he had fallen. His first thought was a rattlesnake den, and he froze sharply.

He listened carefully, choking screams in his throat. He thought at any moment he would hear the slumbering serpents come alive and shake the dust from their rattles in a terrible chorus. He could see nothing in the crushing black, and could only imagine.

He waited to hear the slithering of their scales sliding roughly over pebbles and dirt, their tongues flicking and probing for him in the dark. His brain pictured them rolling over him, terribly caressing and tickling his body with chills.

Except none of that happened. He could hear nothing, felt nothing around him.

When the fear of this horrible fantasy had melted away, the pain in his mangled leg came rushing back. He howled. He shrieked and cursed. He screamed at the darkness until his throat was raw.

When his pained shouts died to grim sobs, he craned his neck to look back at where he had fallen in. He could barely see anything behind the twists and turns of the burrow, only a faint glow of the moonlight upon the snow outside.

He tried to pull himself back up the steep and winding cavern. He grasped at a root and pulled with all of his might, but then, he felt his leg shift inside of him. This new and sickening pain brought whatever notions of escape he'd had to a screeching halt.

He cried out again. He thought of his now certain fate and how Goddamn unfair it was.

He sobbed as his mind conjured images of freezing to death and his carcass being picked clean by whatever may come upon him.

In the short span of a mere instance, he had been condemned to die in this freezing pit of earth, alone.

Except, he wasn't alone.

He heard it then. Something was awakening, but it wasn't rattlesnakes. It wasn't rabbits or varmints and it wasn't a nest of rats.

Something had begun to stir deeper in the pit, something that chittered and clicked as it stretched its muscles from slumber.

This something was big, he could hear heavy legs scratching and pawing at the ground. But even worse, whatever had begun to wake, was not alone. Whatever that thing was that lived in this cursed pit, had family, and they had all begun to rise.

With hands that shook violently, Miller grabbed at his coat and searched for his matches. In the confusion he had temporarily forgotten them, but he needed them now. He needed to see into this dark abyss that bathed him with horror. The unknown was almost certainly worse than whatever lay beyond.

With trembling hands he found the matches, wrestled one out and struck it.

The black void dissipated and he saw what unholy creature had just awoken from its hibernation.

It was more horrible than he could have ever imagined.

Bryant Boothe awoke in his tent to Hal Douglas walking through the entrance flap, Delbert McKinley at his side. Bryant squinted against the beam of light that dashed under the tent flap, before it was closed again. He rubbed his eyes.

"Morning boys." Bryant said as he rolled to a sitting position on the bed. He stood and reached down for his trousers that had been crumpled on the floor. He was halfway through the second leg of the pants, and standing on one foot when Hal spoke.

"Elliot's dead."

Ice filled Bryant's heart immediately. "What? Where did... How?"

Hal looked Bryant dead in the eyes while he spoke, not resigning his gaze to the floor, even though he very much wanted to. "Davey found him this morning. He'd been missing three days."

"Three days." Bryant exhaled painfully. "Why didn't you tell me?"

Hal shrugged sorrowfully. "I wanted to give it time. Figured he needed to blow off steam. He looked ready to pop when we last saw him."

"You should've told me!" Bryant exclaimed.

Hal gave into the urge to cast his eyes down this time. "You're right. I made a mistake."

Bryant, still processing the news of his baby brother, felt worse at the downtrodden look of his right hand man. He stifled tears that wanted to come and breathed quietly for a moment. "How did it happen?"

"Davey found him a couple miles away from that fort." Delbert said, speaking up for the first time.

Bryant buried his face in his hands and shook his head at the confirmation of what he'd already known. "That Goddamn fool." Bryant said; more to himself than the others. "Them two at the fort then? Those ones that killed Elton and Charlie when Elliot tried to shake them down?"

"Best we figure." Hal said. "What do you wanna do?"

"I wanna see him." Bryant said, and moved to get his coat.

"We already buried him." Hal replied, wincing at what was to come.

"What?" Bryant asked dumbfounded.

Hal looked up again at Bryant, communicating with his eyes and the pain and seriousness behind them. "He was shot to hell. I thought it best you didn't see." Hal swallowed. "I've got his hat and boots back on my bedroll. In the case that you wanted to hold your own service."

Bryant half scowled and half pulled his face into a silent sob. "You put my baby brother in the dirt. You put him in there without me."

"It was my decision. If it was wrong, I will take that with me." Hal spoke.

"Was anyone else with him? Did he go alone?" Bryant asked.

Delbert spoke up. "That Pataky boy is missing too. He might've gone, but he ain't turned up yet. He could be lying low someplace."

Bryant nodded, his face twisted into a grimace to force back the pain. He was quiet for a moment, as he walked to a small desk that was set against the side of the tent.

"Look what we've been reduced to." Bryant sighed and then seemingly snapped an instant later. He yelled and flipped the desk, the contents spilled and rolled on the floor.

"We were The Great Dan Crowder Gang! We're the Bryant Boothe gang! We've lived like kings! Outlaw kings! Now look at us. Hiding up in the mountains and trees like some quivering pup!"

Bryant kicked the desk in between his words, accentuating his shouts with bangs on the wood. "My own brother murdered by some damn pioneer peckerwoods! Goddammit!"

A growing murmur was building up outside the tent now, as the camp gathered around to listen in on the commotion.

With a loud sniff and a paw at his disheveled hair that hung in his eyes, Bryant spoke collected. "Get the men all together, we ride to the fort tonight. We will remind these people of the respect we deserve."

"Do we really need that noise?" Delbert interjected, immediately regretting having done so.

Bryant looked at him through fire in his eyes. "What?"

Delbert stammered a moment. "I mean, we don't know what we're getting into. We're supposed to be lying low, I thought. Boss, you know I didn't rightly care for your brother, but I'm just trying to think."

Bryant had walked to Delbert now, who grew quieter and quieter with each step.

Delbert cleared his throat. "It's a shame and all, but Elliot was a hothead. He might've gotten what was coming to him."

Bryant socked him in the nose. Delbert went stumbling backwards and landed on his ass, his head sitting in between the flaps of the tent. The fabric flaps draped over his head like comical hair while his nose bled.

"You forget your place." Bryant said. "Do as I say and gather the men." Bryant walked forward, already regretting losing his temper at Delbert. He bent over and extended him a hand.

Delbert cautiously took it, wondering if another punch was in the mail. Bryant helped him up.

"I didn't want to do that. But you made me. Clean yourself up and go do as I say." Bryant instructed, as he used Delbert's shirt to wipe the blood off of his own knuckles. He patted Delbert on the shoulders, who nodded shakily and left.

Bryant turned to Hal who watched him cautiously but had a twinge of shame behind his eyes. Bryant shook it off, hating himself for doing something so rash in front of the wise, old, Hal Douglas.

"Anything for me boss?" Hal asked dryly.

Bryant nodded. "Get someone else and see if you can round up that Pataky boy before we ride. If he's still alive, I wanna know what he knows."
Hal nodded and left Bryant.

The powerful and brave Bryant Boothe. The man who had cracked a shot at a gang of outlaws when he was just a boy. The man who now stood in the wreckage of his room, knuckles stinging and feeling like a fool with a loose temper.

"I'll make it right little brother." Bryant spoke to himself. Hating, but justifying his actions quietly, he finished getting dressed and went outside.

Chapter 10

Slowly, Abraham opened his eyes. Sun was trickling in from the outside and he breathed in slowly. He allowed himself a slight smile. This was the most peaceful he had awoken in a long time.

His stomach wasn't full, but it didn't gnaw and curdle like it had been. Buchanan and himself had had the fine luck of bagging two rabbits a day prior.

He lay on the floor, his bedroll spread out near the table that had become his. He could hear Buchanan snoring still, and he lay quietly in this brief moment of solitude and calm. The moment of calm that was not unlike the beginning of morning for many others.

The short time when the comfort of sleep and the revitalization of rest temporarily clouds all the tasks of the day, all the worries and pain. That brief feeling of pure contentment, when one is allowed to wake up on one's own terms.

Abraham did not think of the perilous situation they found themselves in, nor the loss of their comrades. Not anything, for the time being.

The mind is a blank slate for approximately sixty seconds in the early waking hours, and it is one of the best feelings in the world.

As he gradually woke, he looked up at the ceiling, glancing over the knots and cracks in the wood. Finally, with a grunt and clearing his throat as he did so, he sat up. He stretched out his arms and yawned, a yawn that was cut short by what he saw.

Caleb was sitting up in his bed, completely on his own. The boy looked confused, peering out through falling hairs and wrapped bandages.

Abraham rubbed his eyes and blinked, certain that he must still be asleep.

Caleb turned to him then, his voice deep and hoarse from its little use during his recovery. "Abraham?"

Abraham shot to his feet. "Caleb! Oh thank God." He rushed to the young man and wrapped his arms around him in a strong embrace.

Caleb jumped a little as the man crushed him in a bear hug. He raised an eyebrow for a moment, but then returned the embrace.

"How are you feeling?" Abraham asked.

Caleb rubbed one of his eyes. "Hungry. Sore."

Abraham nodded and rushed outside. He returned a moment later with the leftover, uncooked rabbit they had saved out in the cold. He went tending to the shimmering coals of the fire, stoking it. He started the rabbit and went back to Caleb as it unthawed and began to cook.

"Here." Abraham said, handing a cup to Caleb. "Drink this."

Caleb accepted the cup, swirling it as he took a look at it.

"Water." Abraham said.

Caleb nodded and downed the cup in several large gulps. "So much seems like a dream. How long have we been here?" He asked.

Abraham half shrugged, slightly embarrassed. "We've both kind of lost track. A couple of weeks at least. I think..."

Caleb considered this with another nod, squinting one eye. He turned to see Mr. Buchanan who still snored at his side, regarded him, and turned back to Abraham. "Did the soldiers agree to help?"

Abraham looked perplexed for a moment, then understood. "There were no soldiers. The place was abandoned. It's just us." He said quietly.

Caleb turned half a frown, but seemed to have expected this a little bit himself. "We'd better head back then. Clanton'll need our help, soldiers or not."

Abraham's eyes flashed pain for a moment, then, he nodded and placed a hand on Caleb's shoulder. "We will. But not til we're sure you've recovered fully. That old bible thumper can make due without us til then."

"Oh I'll be fine." Caleb protested, still very visibly pale and weak.

Then, Buchanan awoke. A choked snore brought the man to a sitting position. He floated open his eyes and jumped a little when he saw Abraham sitting there, face to face with him.

"Christ." Buchanan coughed out. He stood then, hacking his lungs and scratching his netherregions.

Abraham looked to Buchanan and then back to Caleb. "Mr. Buchanan. Caleb has recovered."

Buchanan offered little more than a glance. He looked at Caleb and nodded his head. "Well, good to have you back boy. It's been tough going without you." He walked to the door and popped it open.

As it swung shut, they could hear him spitting wads of phlegm and taking an intermittent piss.

Abraham looked at Caleb and nearly cracked up, the absurdity and obliviousness to norms never stopped with observation of Buchanan.

Then, he remembered the rabbit. He hopped to his feet and retrieved it. Setting it on a plate, he cut it into

smaller chunks and returned to the bed. As he assisted
Caleb with eating, Buchanan returned and walked back to
the bed to retrieve his boots.

His nose crinkled as he caught a whiff of the rabbit,
and he turned. "Oh good." He said, reaching for a chunk.
"You've made breakfast."

Abraham swatted his hand away.

Buchanan scowled angrily. "Do not strike me like I
am some sort of house pet."

"Caleb needs all he can get." Abraham replied,
holding the plate away.

Buchanan huffed a dry and sarcastic chuckle. "We
cannot afford special privileges or considerations, Mr.
Mercer. We all need to eat. Yourself included."

Abraham still held the plate away, before Caleb
placed a hand on his arm, lowering it.

"He's right." The young man said.

Buchanan retrieved his piece and stuffed it into his
mouth. He chewed it minimally and swallowed it,
continuing to get dressed. "Mr. Mercer. Get ready, we've
got to go out."

Abraham let the plate drop to Caleb's lap, who ate
his portion slowly.

"Where are we going?" Abraham asked.

Buchanan cleared his throat again and spit into the open door of the stove. His saliva sizzled on the coals.

"Well, since the boy's up and at 'em, and since that's the last of the rabbit, we gotta find something more. I reckon we give the cabins another "once over". Let's see if there's anything we've missed."

Abraham thought for a moment, then agreed.

He left the plate with Caleb and stood. Mouthing the words: "You can have mine." so Buchanan wouldn't hear, he walked back to his things and began to get dressed.

Moments later, Buchanan was out the door with Abraham at his rear.

"Abraham?" A voice called from the bed.

Abraham turned and looked back at Caleb.

Caleb used his eyes to flick to the bedpan against the wall, embarrassment in his expression.

Abraham nodded discreetly. "Buchanan I'll be just a moment." He called outside, and closed the door.

Buchanan replied with something murmured and unintelligible outside, and Abraham walked to assist Caleb.

They had cleared two of the buildings and had found nothing. Well, nothing aside from some more fabric and blankets.

Now they had come to the last cabin. The place Abraham had found the journal and the chest full of food scraps.

They entered the door and the place was exactly as they had left it; dingy, dusty and unremarkable.

They went through the motions, neither of them expecting to find much, and they didn't.

As they were about to leave, Buchanan spotted a hat atop a high shelf that he hadn't noticed before.

"I like the looks of that hat." He remarked and had walked toward the shelf, standing on his tiptoes to admire it.

Abraham turned and looked at it, and then to Buchanan. "Think this fella had something squirreled away there too?" He asked.

Buchanan turned to face Abraham, a foolish half-grin on his face. "No. I just like the hat." He said seriously as he reached up behind him, not looking at it and pulled it down.

Three solid objects hit the floor, one after the other as Buchanan pulled the hat from its perch.

CLACK. CLACK. CLACK.

They looked down dismissively at whatever had clattered to the floor and froze in their tracks.

Dynamite.

Yes, Goddamn Dynamite. Three sticks had clattered to the floor and by some divine intervention, or a once in a lifetime miracle, they had not exploded.

Abraham stared at them, watching one roll along the uneven floor and finally come to rest against the wall. Buchanan looked too, semi-certain that he had slightly shit his pants.

"Is that what I think it is?" Abraham asked quietly, almost in a near whisper.

Buchanan nodded. "It sure is."

Abraham breathed out slowly. "I might vomit."

Buchanan raised his hand slowly to quiet Abraham and looked down at the charges.

"We should be halfway to heaven right now. Plain and simple. It's a Goddamn miracle that we aren't in a million pieces." Buchanan whispered, as if a loud tone would offend the nitroglycerin, causing it to lose its temper and erupt.

"What do we do?" Abraham hissed over at him.

Buchanan pulled one of the rolls of fabric from his pack and looked to Abraham for confirmation before he tossed it to him.

"Pick 'em up." Buchanan said as calmly as he could. "As gentle as you can. Like eggs."

"Yeah. Eggs that'll blow us to kingdom come." Abraham thought to himself, before he shot back an angry; "Why me?!"

Buchanan scowled back and hissed. "You've got steadier hands. You've seen how mine shake."

"My ass!" Abraham shouted back.

Buchanan waved his hands in an exasperated motion. "Just do it!" He ordered through his teeth.

Abraham swallowed and licked his lips. He spread the cloth out in his open palm and slowly lowered himself toward the floor. He reached cautiously with a hand that was trembling terribly, moving toward the closest stick.

"Molasses like." Buchanan offered as he watched.

Abraham's hand stopped just short of the charge, jumping at Buchanan's unsolicited advice. "Would you shut your cock-holster for one minute?!" He shouted back with a frazzled and shaking voice.

Buchanan nodded and made a gesture of the buttoning of the lip.

Abraham reached the stick again and grasped it with three fingers. Thumb, middle, and pointer gripped the stick and brought it gently to rest in his palm.

Buchanan breathed out and wiped his forehead as he observed.

Abraham retrieved the other in a similar fashion, wincing as it clicked against the other charge already in his palm.

As he crawled on hand and knees toward the final stick, something gave way on the floor and he fell forward. Barely, he managed to soften the tremor and hold his hand up from the ground as his face mashed into the wood.

Buchanan audibly gasped and it was Abraham's turn to soil his pants slightly.

After a moment of gathering, Abraham picked himself back up slowly and crawled again toward the final charge.

What he didn't notice in this painfully slow, battle against eruption, was that what had tripped him was a floorboard.

Not a loose floorboard, but a deliberate floorboard. A board that had been removed very carefully and placed back again just as cautiously, to conceal something underneath its inconspicuous surface.

None of this mattered to Abraham in this moment of course. Nor did Buchanan notice as Abraham's knee left the upturned board and the wood clattered back into its watchful spot as sentry. Whatever had been hidden in this compartment would maintain its confidentiality, for now.

At last, the third and final stick was brought to rest against its two siblings, and was covered gently in the folds of the cloth.

Abraham stood, looking to Buchanan as he held a literal time bomb in his hands. "Now what?"

Buchanan thought for a moment. "Take it out where you buried that stiff. Far away from here."

Abraham recoiled, dumbfounded. "Do you know how far that is?!" He whispered out angrily.

"If it goes off. It can't go off near here. For a myriad of reasons. I have no clue how old that is, how unstable." Buchanan reasoned, thinking aloud.

"You don't say!" Abraham shot back. "I ain't walking through sticks and rocks with the fires of hell set to explode in my hands!"

Buchanan raised his hands in surrender. "I'll go with you." He stammered. "How's that?"

Abraham stared at him with wide and angry eyes. A moment later he swallowed before saying; "Well, let's go then!"

And so they had.

Buchanan had held the door for him, as Abraham had waddled through, holding his hands as far from himself as he could manage. It was as if he had wrestled a lethal cobra into his grasp and could not give even an inch to the filthy serpent.

Painstakingly, for what seemed like days, they had walked. No, they had crawled. Step by step, they had made it inch by inch away from the fort.

Once, as Abraham had waited for Buchanan to open the gate, his nose had begun to itch something terrible. His eyes watered and his nerves begged him to scratch it, but he had not relented.

Now, after a painfully long time, they had arrived at the drift where Clifford had been buried.

Abraham couldn't have told the burial site from a shit house in normal circumstances, but wind had revealed puffs of colored uniform and frozen bony fingers.

With arms and hands that begged and pleaded for rest, he set the parcel of hell upon the snow and carefully stepped back.

When they had both retreated away from the dynamite more than 100 yards, they both sucked in a collective sigh of relief.

"God in heaven." Buchanan had remarked.

Abraham vomited the near nothingness of his stomach onto the snow with painful wretches. He spit out the taste of bile and sucked in a gasp of air. When he stood, he looked to Buchanan. Curiously, Buchanan was looking past him.

Buchanan had his pistol drawn and had it seemingly aimed right at Abraham.

"What...What are you doing?" Abraham asked in a confused near-whisper.

"Get down. Be quiet." Buchanan whispered out, his gaze flicking to something behind Abraham.

Slowly, Abraham turned and looked at what the target truly was.

A very small deer, either an older fawn, or a doe that was a runt, was standing in the clearing at their rear.

Abraham's breath caught in his throat and he fought back the reflex of surprise, ducking his head.

With one eye closed, Buchanan aimed with still slightly trembling hands at the deer that was nearly sixty yards away. Not an easy shot for a pistol, and one he was not confident to gamble on. He lowered his hand, his stomach hating him for it.

"What are you doing?" Abraham whispered with an angry confusion. "Take the shot!"

Buchanan shook his head softly. "Too far. I ain't sure I could hit it. We need to get closer."

Abraham turned his head to look at the deer again, and jumped in fright when out of nowhere, an arrow sailed into the deer's side.

Both of these men, neither of them strangers to attacks by Indian war parties, reflexively ducked behind the nearest cover before they even thought about it.

Buchanan whispered a "psst!" to Abraham, and then tossed him his second pistol.

Abraham caught it, his head on fire with adrenaline and a knot tightening in his gut. He was ducked behind a tree that was slightly more elevated than the one Buchanan hid behind. He could see the dying and collapsed deer, Buchanan could not.

"What do you see?" Buchanan whispered.

Abraham squinted his eyes over the shimmering snow. The deer was felled on the ground, but no one had come to finish it yet. The pitiful thing was bellowing softly and leaking its crimson life onto the ground with rising steam.

"Nothing yet." Abraham whispered back. "Just the fawn."

Buchanan nodded, considering this information. "I'm gonna move closer. Keep an eye out." He began to stand slowly but was halted by a hasty hand motion from Abraham.

"Wait. Wait. Something's coming out of the trees." Abraham said.

Abraham watched, as out of the trees The Rogue emerged. He was painted in white ash on both his skin and clothes and was incredibly hard to see as he walked to the dying deer. Even though Abraham had only barely caught a glimpse of this man once before, he knew immediately who it was.

"Oh my God." Abraham breathed.

"What?!" Buchanan hissed.

"It's the Goddamn rogue."

Buchanan looked slightly confused for a moment, but then understood. "Keep an eye on him." Buchanan instructed. "I'm gonna creep up on him."

"No." Abraham exhaled and raised Buchanan's pistol. "I've got him."

"No you don't!" Buchanan whispered angrily. "Put down the gun you Goddamn fool!"

Abraham wasn't listening, he was zeroed in. He had the butcher that had maimed Caleb in his sights, and his finger on the trigger.

The Rogue was now crouched next to the deer and had begun to dress it.

Abraham exhaled, taking into account every slight breeze and twitch of his muscles. But, just as he had begun to send the signal from brain to finger and started to squeeze the trigger, The Rogue had sensed them.

Something, some sound that was inaudible to the two men, had perked up The Rogue's ears. Abruptly, he had drawn an arrow at unbelievable speed, nocked it, drawn it and fired.

The arrow sailed into the tree Abraham was covering himself with, narrowly missing its mark of his face.

Abraham jumped back, turning sideways and accidentally pulling the trigger. The shot cracked off and exploded just over Buchanan's head.

Buchanan dove his face into the snow in reflex, as the bullet zipped by his head.

Abraham took a moment to collect himself, as he navigated through the shock of narrowly avoiding death. Then, he dove back out, hammer cocked and ready to fire.

The Rogue was gone, seemingly vanished into thin air.

"Dammit!" Abraham yelled. He scanned the trees and snow for the ash-white silhouette of the ghost.

Nothing.

Buchanan had stood and walked to Abraham's side. "Give me my pistol, you blockhead." He said with an extended hand.

Abraham sighed loudly, both in anger and embarrassment. He lowered the hammer on the dragoon and passed it sheepishly to Buchanan. He stood, dusting snow from himself and felt his face growing red.

"He's gone." Abraham said angrily.

"No shit." Buchanan scolded. "Listen to your elders next time."

"I had him. I don't know how he saw me." Abraham said to himself.

"Mystic are the ways of the Injun." Buchanan said, returning his pistol to its holster. "Still, there are silver linings to your foolishness."

"What's that?" Abraham asked sarcastically.

"Well he left the deer. Way I see it, it's ours now." Buchanan replied, looking across the clearing to the kill.

Sometime later, after they had brought the fawn back to the fort, they had hung the deer in the cook's station, cleaned it and drained it. Now, the meat was cooking on a spit at the courtyard campfire.

It hadn't been difficult bringing it back. The creature was quite pitiful and no self respecting sportsman would have even considered killing it. But to three starving men, it might as well have been choice cuts of the finest beev.

Abraham had assisted Caleb to the table and they now sat, anxiously awaiting the meal that Buchanan was preparing just outside.

"How're you feeling?" Abraham asked.

"Alright." Caleb replied. "Still real sore. A little foggy too." Caleb laughed, quietly to himself. "You think Clanton will believe it when I tell him? That I almost got scalped by a real-life injun and lived?"

Abraham swallowed back the truth again. "It's a hell of a tale." He replied.

"I don't even know how bad it looks, and it was the most painful thing I've ever been through. But that's the kind of tale you read in one of them dime novels. "Caleb Bradley; the half scalped mountain man and his daring pursuits." Caleb laughed a little again.

Abraham smiled too, a feeling of sadness twinging in his mind. Caleb was still just a kid in so many ways.

"Don't get a swelled head now." Abraham reasoned jokingly. "You'll pop the scar before it sets." He shook his head to himself, cringing at the mediocre wisecrack.

Caleb nodded, grinning. But then, his grin faltered, and he grew serious as he went somewhere in his head.

"You know... It's kinda funny the way things happen. When I seen what they'd done to Bill those years ago, it always came up in my nightmares."

"Bill?" Abraham inquired. "That the name of the one legged trapper?"

Caleb nodded, distant in thought, and somber. "That was always the most grisly thing I'd ever seen. Worst thing that could pop into my mind at any time. Kinda funny that I was afraid of that for so long and it happened to me."

Abraham didn't know what to say to this. He thought for a moment, but resigned to simply placing a hand on Caleb's shoulder. "You're one tough kid Caleb."

"I ain't no kid. I'll be eighteen this year and I been a man since long before that." The kid replied defensively.

Abraham grinned, raising his hands up in a comical surrender. "You're right. You're right. I apologize for the offense, mister."

Caleb grinned and grew red. "Oh shut your trap, old man."

"I mean it mister." Abraham continued, making his voice high-pitched and quivering. "I won't never offend the big ole' Caleb Bradley again."

Caleb rolled his eyes and shook his head, a smile battling to come through on his lips.

Buchanan kicked the door open. Steaming meat was piled on a plate in his hands.

Abraham and Caleb watched as Buchanan stumbled in, carrying the plate carefully. The smell hit them at once and their stomachs leapt in anticipation.

To a well fed man, this meal would seem grim. There was a lack of any seasoning besides some salt, and the meat was gamy to the taste. The fawn was young and sinewy. Its tough and wiry muscle would have been better suited to a slow cooked stew if anything.

But these men had gone hungry for many days and nights, subsisting on dry flour biscuits and scraps. And so tonight, they would eat meat piled high on a plate, like men.

Buchanan set the plate in the middle of the table and sat down.

"If Clanton were here he'd be knocking us over the head until we said grace." Caleb said.

Buchanan raised an eyebrow and looked to Abraham who greeted him with wide and pleading eyes. Buchanan closed his half-open mouth, and understood. "You're right, kid. It'll please the preacher, even in his absence." He said with a minimal grin. "Why don't you do it then?"

Caleb nodded with a smile and interlocked his fingers. With a bowed head, he led the men in a prayer.

"Dear lord. We thank thee for this bountiful meal. We thank thee for your grace in helping us survive. We ask that you watch over your man Clanton and the rest of his flock. In the name of our lord. Amen."

"Amen." The men said in unison.

They began to dig in. With the lack of any other courses, they simply ripped pieces off the main plate and ate them out of their hands.

Juices dripped down their chins, as they chewed and savored the meat. They chewed and chewed, neglecting to swallow until they had obliterated each bite in their mouths. Grunts of pleasure and enjoyment were sounded as each bite was taken.

Buchanan stood abruptly. He wiped his chin and began to walk.

"What is it?" Abraham asked with a mouthful of food, and a large hunk of deer still in his hands.

"Hold on a moment." Buchanan said. He walked to the bed and kneeled.

A trick floorboard wiggled with prodding from Buchanan, he grabbed the edge and lifted it. Out of the hole, he withdrew a large bottle of whiskey.

"Where'd you get that?" Abraham asked with raised eyes.

"I found it a while ago. Been saving it for either emergency or maybe the elusive celeration." Buchanan said as he uncorked it and took a swig. "Might be our last good time for a while. We may as well enjoy it." He passed the bottle to Abraham who paused, and looked it over for a moment. He relented with a grin and drank it, passing it back to Buchanan.

"It ain't my turn." Buchanan said, rejecting the bottle and passing it to Caleb. "Drink up boy."

Caleb looked back to Buchanan and then to Abraham, eyes wide and grinning wildly. He tilted back the bottle and took entirely too large of a gulp.

Caleb's eyes grew wide and he yanked the bottle from his lips with a choked yelp. His throat was alight with a raging inferno. His eyes watered and his nose ran.

Buchanan tilted back his head and howled with laughter. Abraham chuckled with a hand over his mouth.

"Damnation!" Caleb shouted with a slap of his hand on the table. "That hurt like hell."

"But you've been drinking spirits for weeks." Abraham interjected as he considered the thought.

Caleb looked at him with genuine bemusement. "I have? I sure as hell don't remember that." Caleb coughed again. "Nothing that hurt like that anyway."

Buchanan shrugged. "I'd been watering it down after the first couple of days. Didn't know how long we'd need it."

Abraham shot his gaze to him, growing angry for a moment. "You what? You had a full bottle stashed and you were watering down medicine for the sick?!" He burst out.

"Hey, Abraham." Caleb interjected, trying to diffuse the fight before it started. "It's okay. I'm alright now."

Abraham quieted a moment, considering this. He scowled, wanting to reprimand Buchanan further. But up until this moment, the night had been pleasant, happy even. As irritated as he was with the situation, he decided it could wait.

Buchanan looked back at him and awaited the next words.

Abraham sighed. "I suppose it worked out. But no more secrets."

Buchanan nodded and crossed his heart in a mockingly exaggerated motion. "Never again."

Then, with filling bellies and an ever increasing intake of whiskey, the spat was forgotten. On and on the night had carried, bringing with it many bursts of uproarious laughter, and deafening claps of the hands.

Several games of blackjack were played after Buchanan had taught Caleb the game.

"You get a seventeen and you don't hit. Don't let any fool convince you otherwise. But, you get a sixteen, hit every time cause you're up shit-creek either way." Buchanan had said with a laugh as Caleb had studied the cards.

They had played without any form of wager. The only thing that had value in this place was food. But they all had full bellies now, with none left to bet.

They simply kept track of how many hands each of them had won against the rotating dealer. A tally that was blurred and quickly forgotten with each additional swig from the bottle.

Another bottle had appeared at some point. Abraham, now too drunk to question the means that this bottle had come into existence by, drank it happily and returned to the poker game that they were now playing.

Hours and hours had passed. The night had grown older and now Abraham and Buchanan were in the midst of a drunken and rambling story.

Caleb was face down on the table, snoring.

"My Mama…" Abraham said with a hiccup. He belched and swallowed back a half-food and half-whiskey mixture before continuing.

"She was so Goddamn mad at my Daddy after that. I never seen her that angry. Madder than a wet cat." He paused, taking another drink and grimacing at the burn. "Well, when he was out working one day, she got his long-johns and sewed the crap flap shut. She even double seamed it."

Buchanan spit out a drunken and wheezy laugh, Abraham joined him.

After they had quieted again, Abraham continued. His words were slurring and at times nearly unintelligible.

"Even then when I was that young, I knew what was to come. I waited outside, by the shit house all day. My Daddy kept coming up to me asking "What in the sam-hell I was doing." I could barely hold in my giggles. And then, when nature finally called and he brought open that door and stepped inside, I ran up and listened." Abraham laughed wheezily. "God damn. Ain't no one ever heard sounds like the ones I heard that day. Lots of; "What in the good Goddamn!?" and "That infernal woman!" But the funniest thing were his grunts that grew more and more panicked by the second. There was a reckoning coming and my Daddy couldn't get the door open."

Buchanan slapped the table, almost hard enough to crack the wood and cackled like a witch. Somehow, this didn't wake Caleb who snored drunkenly in his own drool.

"Many noises transpired in there." Abraham continued. "But ultimately, my Daddy walked down to the creek with shame, head hung low like a dog."

They laughed for a long time. Laughed so long they couldn't nearly breathe. After the thunderous howling had finally subsided, their attention turned to Caleb, who acknowledged their gaze with a hearty snort, followed by more loud snoring.

Abraham blinked drunkenly and began to stand. "We should get this one to bed."

Buchanan waved a hand and took another drink. "Let him learn. Every man needs a night spent at a table. Builds character."

Abraham shook his head. "Oh I'll do it you old drunkard." He spoke dismissively and stooped down to pick up the kid. He hefted the boy up who was much heavier than he looked. Abraham bobbed and swayed as he lifted and hoisted. He stumbled a moment, nearly careening to the floor with the kid in his arms. After some laborious and grunt filled movements, he had laid the boy upon the bed.

Abraham collapsed onto his ass and followed it with wheezing laughter. He stood and meandered back over to the table with Buchanan.

"Whew boy." Abraham sighed as he sat down. "We're running low on drink. You got any more secret liquor stowed?"

Buchanan shook his head. "Not that I can recall presently."

"That's probably for the best." Abraham sighed and laid his head back, staring at the ceiling. He raised his head again and looked at Buchanan. "You know…"

Whatever Abraham had meant to say was quickly cut off and forgotten. A gunshot had suddenly ripped through the air outside and jolted both men in shock.

Buchanan had drawn his pistols reflexively and had his ears perked and open. Abraham had drunkenly scrambled to the wall where his rifle leaned.

He had nearly crashed face first into the wall, but he had retrieved the firearm and now held it, awaiting further information.

Outside, a muffled voice shouted from beyond the perimeter wall. "You men in the fort! Come out!"

"Who in the hell is that?" Abraham asked Buchanan with slurred words.

"Shhh!!" Buchanan scolded as he listened.

"Get out right now! Or we will light you up!" The voice called again.

Buchanan stood and stumbled to the door. After a moment of navigating the intricacies of the basic wooden opening, he managed to open it and waddle outside.

Abraham had jumped to his feet at the rear and had followed haphazardly. "Wait up!" He called ahead.

"You all in the fort!" The voice shouted again.

Abraham had come out into the courtyard now. He stumbled out into the snow and the door slammed shut behind him.

Buchanan whipped around, eyes wide and glassy with drink. "Quiet dammit!" He hissed out in a whisper.

Buchanan then collided loudly with an empty barrel. He fell ass over teakettle.

The barrel tipped and rolled, bumping over rocks and jostling to a stop against the gate.

Outside, Bryant Boothe grinned. "So you are home." He said to himself. "Come out now Goddammit!" He called to the dark fort.

No response.

"Very well!" Bryant cleared his throat.

"Five!"

Inside, Buchanan and Abraham had stumbled to the gate. They peered out cautiously through the slats and looked outside. Just on the other side of the gate, ten or more men on horseback waited. Torches, held by some of the men illuminated the posse in a hellish and orange glow.

"Four!" Bryant called out.

Buchanan held his pistols and thought quietly to himself. Abraham was at his side, wide eyed and waiting for some sort of instruction. Buchanan blinked heavily, trying to find some sort of constructive thought in the scrambled and drunken haze his mind had been reduced to.

"Three!" Bryant called.

Abraham shook Buchanan's shoulder. The old bounty hunter looked at him and gave a wide eyed and raised-eyebrow stare.

Abraham raised and lowered his shoulders dramatically, as if to say: "*Well, what in the goddamn fuck are we supposed to do now?*"

"Two!" Bryant shouted.

"We're here!" Buchanan called out.

Outside, the posse had jumped a little at the sudden response from the quiet structure. Bryant grinned to himself and was quiet for a moment. A few seconds later he replied. "So you are here!"

Buchanan thought for a moment and shouted back. "No disrespect here sir! But who do I have the pleasure of addressing!?"

Bryant sighed. "Bryant Boothe! And the Bryant Boothe gang! We've got you surrounded!"

Buchanan nodded, slightly amused to himself. "Ah! I thought we would be making your acquaintance at some point!" He called back.

Bryant scowled at the insubordinate tone that had shouted at him from the dark. He swallowed rage and the urge to tell his men to fill the decrepit fort full of holes.

"Ah!" Bryant called back. "So you'd be the bastard that killed my brother then!"

Buchanan shook his head dramatically, as if Bryant could see him. "No sir!" He shouted. "But I believe I have him here with me! Shall I introduce the two of you!?"

Bryant dropped his head. He bit his cheeks in anger at the nearly mocking voice that he was conversating with. "Goddamn peckerwood." He murmured to himself. Then, he raised his head again and yelled. "Yes!"

Buchanan looked to his side at Abraham. He tilted his head toward the outside of the fort as if to say: "*Well, that's your cue!*"

Abraham responded with an unbelieving and wide-eyed expression that said: "*Is this really your brilliant plan??*"

Abraham shook his head, not quite believing he was here. Through a vague sobriety, brought on by the cold and adrenaline, he mustered his voice and quelled the slurring. "This is Abraham Mercer!" He called out. "I killed your brother!"

Bryant scowled, nostrils flaring and teeth grinding. "Come out then!" He called. "I'd sure love to make your acquaintance in person!" He snorted in and cast out a ball of mucous. "Come on out Abraham!"

Abraham tightened his grip on the rifle and swallowed. He thought quietly for a moment on a response, but Buchanan delivered it for him.

"He only killed him cause your brother killed his friends! Our friends! Butchered a whole Goddamn wagon train!"

"The wagon party?" Bryant thought to himself, considering this new information. "That Goddamn fool. He don't deserve the vengeance I'm seeking for him."

Bryant cleared his throat. "I don't know nothing about that! But you! Old fella, this don't concern you! You send Abraham out to us and we'll leave you and yours be!"

Buchanan frowned. "Old fella?" He murmured. He pulled back the hammers on his guns and slid his back up the wall of the fort as he stood. "Well Mr. Boothe! You drive a hard bargain!" Buchanan shouted out into the night. "We're coming out!"

Abraham looked wide-eyed to Buchanan from his sitting position in the snow. He opened his hands slightly around the rifle and raised his eyebrows, awaiting something, anything.

"Don't worry." Buchanan whispered. "I've got a plan."

Then, not a moment later, all hell broke loose.

Inside, Buchanan and Abraham could not tell exactly what was happening, just on the other side of the wall, but they could hear it. At the sudden clamor of commotion they had fallen back to their positions against the fence and could now only sit, frozen in their swirling and drunken state.

One of Bryant's men outside had first begun shouting incoherently at his partners. His attention was at the edge of the woods. He was witnessing something unrecognizable, something that nearly broke his brain. As his eyes tried to communicate to his mind what exactly he was seeing, he had only managed confused and terrified yelps.

This had pulled the other mens' attention to the forest also, just in time to see what 'something awful' was bearing down on them.

And oh boy was it; 'something awful' and there were so many of them.

Terrified shrieks from the rest of the men followed, accompanied by total calamity. Gunshots rang out, horses screamed and bucked their riders. The stallions fled into the night where they would be picked off later, like the men they had thrown.

Slashing, tearing, ripping...gurgling.

Then there were the shrieks. Not shrieks made by a man as he stared death in the face. Shrieks that were inhuman, otherworldly and terrifying. High pitched screeches, accompanied with yowls and squawks.

These ear piercing calls caused Abraham and Buchanan to clutch their temples, closing their eyes in pain.

The splitting cries would rise and fall until they would drop from the highest peak of pitch, and tumble downward into guttural bellows.

Abraham, fighting the painful ringing in his ears, tilted his head sideways to peer out from one of the slats. Buchanan noticed him, and shifted to do the same.

The view was limited, and they could only see a glimpse into the carnage beyond.

Blood, pieces of people, and horses were strewn about on the ground. Snapped bones protruded from sections of meat. The tender marrow glistened against the light of the dropped torches that still burned against the snow.

The carnage continued.

Abraham and Buchanan tilted their heads this way and that, trying to make out some sort of understanding of what the hell was going on.

Then, one of the men outside fell into view, in the slender frame of the slat. He was bloody, both with his own and that of many others. One of his arms was broken, very badly. The bone was poking out through torn flesh. The arm was dangling and swayed as the man crawled. He dragged himself to the gate, eyes bleary with tears and nose dripping snot.

"Let me in!" He called upward to the gate of the structure. "Dear God, let me in!"

Caught up in the absolutely mind bending chaos, Abraham almost did. He almost jumped to his feet and unlatched the gate. Almost tore open the gate for the broken-armed man and let him in. And let whatever ungodly, and infernal creatures that surrounded, in with him.

But then, in an instant that would be missed with the blink of an eye, something snatched him. Something yanked the broken-armed man out of view and out of existence entirely.

Well, almost entirely. He would continue to exist in one form or another, until the thing that was now audibly chewing on him, had had its fill.

He would continue to exist in an ever diminishing extent, until the buzzards had their turn over the coming days and his bones were bleached by the sun. Until his bones dried completely, cracking and turning entirely to dust.

But, the man that had crawled toward the gate, broken arm swaying and piss running down his legs, that man was dead.

Abraham and Buchanan had known he was dead. They knew the moment they had heard the jaws of the hell incarnate outside close around his throat and cut off his screams.

Many more long minutes later, and all was quiet. Abraham and Buchanan had recoiled away from their peephole as they'd hear the man die. They now stared blankly into the courtyard of the fort, into the void.

They sat with glazed eyes and blank expressions, just staring. The look anyone will have when they have seen something that shatters their entire realm of understanding.

Snow began to fall then. Light flurries at first, and then heavy flakes.

But still, Abraham and Buchanan sat motionless and stared. They stared even as the snow had piled over their clothes and heads. The fire in their bellies and the inferno in their minds would keep them warm for the time being.

For now they sat. They sat until they slept.

Chapter 11

Abraham stirred first. Silently, his eyes opened and for a moment he panicked. He panicked because all he could see was white. He thought for just an instant that he had surely died, and was now in what must be the crushing nothingness that follows death.

He jerked up and watched the nothingness suddenly fall away, revealing the courtyard of the fort.

The courtyard was blanketed in white, a couple feet of snow lay draped over everything, like a heavy quilt. He dug himself out and looked to his side.

There, lay a mound shaped a little like Buchanan. He reached inside the snowy cocoon and stirred the man.

Buchanan awoke with a shout, his head emerging from the icy sarcophagus.

"Easy." Abraham quieted him. "It's just me."

Buchanan hushed after a moment and looked around. He looked confusedly in a few different directions before understanding, and digging himself out.

"I've woken up in worse places I suppose." Buchanan said as he stood, and dusted himself off.

Abraham shook his head. "Foolish of us. We could have frozen to death."

"Not necessarily" Buchanan said, as he blew a rocket of snot out of one nostril. "Snow is a spectacular insulator. Kept us warm as well as an icy blanket can."

Abraham considered this and shrugged. "Did you hear anything else last night?"

Buchanan shook his head. "Nothing. I dozed off not too long after I suppose."

Abraham thought for a moment. "What was..." He began.

Buchanan quieted him with a closed-eye shake of the head. "Do not ask unanswerable questions." He reached into his pocket and fished out the key to the gate. He sighed. "I have seen many strange things in my time. But that last night... has me scared shitless."

He fiddled with the key in his hands a moment longer, before relenting and putting it into the lock on the gate. "Still, I think it best to try and understand what we're up against."

Abraham pulled his face up tight, like he had just eaten something sour. "I don't quite want to. I've seen livestock that were torn apart by beast before." He shuddered. "Gruesome business."

"As have I." Buchanan replied, still holding the key in the lock, immobile. "But I believe there are worse things in store for us out there than grisly sights. I know of no creature in all of creation that sounds, or moves like that. The only thing I know for certain right now, is that there were many of them."

As Buchanan turned the key, an abstract thought landed on Abraham's mind and then fluttered away, like a crow.

"...And into the vastness of the night we shall venture."

He frowned, trying to understand the words that had come into his head out of left-field. But, before he could consider this further, the chain fell to the ground and the gate was creaking open.

"Nothing. No, not nothing." Abraham thought as the gate opened. He looked across the ground outside and tried to understand what he was seeing. "The massacre was smothered by the snow... But where were the mounds and hills where the bodies were buried?"

The snow outside looked untouched, undisturbed. Completely flat, except for some buried tree limbs and rocks.

"I've been prone to nightmares before..." Buchanan began, half-speaking to himself.

Abraham pushed past him and waded out into the den of white. He looked down at his feet, expecting at any moment for the white to be replaced with a frozen and diluted red.

It wasn't.

"Buchanan?!" He called out, frightened. He turned quickly back to the gate, looking for answers. But Buchanan was not looking at him, nor was he looking at the untouched snow.

Buchanan was still standing just before the precipice of the entrance. He looked pale, nervous even. He stared past Abraham and into the foreboding darkness of the trees. He couldn't hear Abraham, he was far away now.

In the same way that a predator will prey on the sick and wounded when it is advantageous to do so, so too will malignant and dark energies. When a mind has been rattled, fatigued, and berated so much that it may finally collapse at any moment, it is very susceptible to persuasion.

Something called out to Buchanan from those darkened pines. Something that had zeroed in on his ever-fraying twine of reality.

It called now. No, it screamed. Over and over in his head, did it scream.

"You will die here. You will die like the filthy soldiers before you. Your kind is a pestilence upon this place. Your life is a boil, prime to be lanced. So do what you always do and hide. Hide and cower from the powers that be, as you continue to prolong the inevitable."

This and many other intrusive words like it, needled into Buchanan's brain with a stabbing ferocity. He took a step back and the signal diminished some.

He took another. Again the signal was weakened. He took several steps back until he could no longer hear the terrible words that had penetrated his mind without his invitation. The voice that was not his, was quieted on the soft ridges of his brain.

The woods grinned at him then. They grinned with sinister viciousness. They grinned and told him; "Yes. Stay in there and hide for now like a good little rabbit. But you will hunger, as all animals do. You will hunger."

Abraham was shaking him now. Buchanan pulled himself back into the chilling present. He looked dazedly at Abraham who was staring intensely at him.

"Did you hear what I said?!" Abraham yelled.

Buchanan furrowed his brow as he pieced his mind back together. "What?" He breathed absently.

"There's nothing!" Abraham shouted and gestured outside the gate.

Buchanan looked out. Abraham had scoured the entire fifty-foot radius the horses had stood on the night before. He had dug down to weeds and dirt in some places. There was nothing, nothing but snow and mud.

"There's no blood! No bodies! Not even horseshit!" Abraham yelled.

Buchanan's heart tumbled down into the recesses of his bowels.

The forest stared at him from beyond the frame of the gate.

"Hide little rabbit. You will hunger."

"What the hell does this mean?!" Abraham shouted.

Buchanan fell to his knees and vomited. After he had spit the last of the sick from his lips, he wiped them. "I need to lie down. I need to rest."

Abraham watched with astounded anger and confusion as Buchanan stood. The old gunfighter wiped the sick from his shirt, dusted himself off and meandered drunkenly back to the cabin.

"No matter." Abraham thought angrily, his head whirling with confusion.

Though, deep down he wanted to do exactly what Buchanan had done. He wanted to go into the bed and throw the covers over his eyes. He wanted to hide like a frightened little boy and not deal with the impossibility of the bare snow outside the gate.

He wouldn't.

A fire had awakened in Abraham, a fire he didn't know that he had ever had. It had been growing the entire journey.

No more than a spark at first, and then gradually an ember, but now it flamed. He would fight tooth and nail to survive and to beat it, though he didn't know how he would.

He turned back toward the open gate and walked outside. He looked around again, his eyes wanting to see something. They wanted to see anything that could quiet the madness that itched at every corner of his mind.

He turned around, and looked over the outside walls of the fort again. This time, he saw it.

There was a blood splatter, painted up the side of the fence that he had not noticed before. He breathed triumphantly, as the madness was pushed back for the time being. But then, he frowned as he looked back at the ground.

Though the blood splatter on the wall confirmed that there had been an attack the night before, the ground didn't. He couldn't figure out why.

There was a piece missing to this puzzle that he worked over in his mind. A piece that when put into place, would finally make the picture clear.

So, he would search for more pieces.

He walked again and again around the perimeter where the men had surrounded the fort the night before. Just as he was about to give up and head inside for the moment, he spotted it.

Tracks.

At first they didn't look like tracks to him. Why would they? They didn't resemble any tracks he or any other man had seen. He bent over and squinted at them, the brightness of the snow blinding him.

The sun was shining brighter and more brilliantly lately, though Abraham wouldn't notice that fact at this moment.

He looked over the tracks again and again.

Yet still, he couldn't say for certain what animal they most resembled. The back of the print resembled the curve of a horse shoe. But the front had imprints of pads; like that of a dog. Then, at the front of the print, deep impressions of long pointed claws.

With the spacing of the tracks, it looked like whatever the creature was, it switched between quadrupedal and bipedal intermittently.

Abraham was no tracker, but he'd picked up a thing or two from some men he'd known, that were. He followed the tracks. Tromping through snow, his eyes glued to the ground, he followed. Track after track came into his vision, and he followed the winding and wandering trail.

At one point, he thought he'd lost it. But then, a moment later, he found it again. He'd found the continuation of the tracks nearly twenty feet from where they'd ended.

"Christ." He thought. "Whatever these things are, they sure can jump far." He shivered at the implications of this information. "If they had heard me or Buchanan, they surely could have leapt the wall with ease."

More and more he walked. Until finally, the tracks did completely up and vanish.

He looked for another continuation but to no avail. He looked up and observed where he was and was surprised.

He hadn't felt that he had walked all that far. But now, he found himself standing at the edge of the forest.

He peered into the rows of pines that stood at attention in winding lines. Like drunken soldiers, these sentries stood their posts, and held the secrets of their home within.

For a moment, he considered heading further inside and trying to pick up the trail again. But, some sort of unconscious instinct changed his mind.

He turned and began to walk back to the fort. He needed to sit. He needed to consider and navigate all that had happened, all the possibilities.

Though something foreign scratched at his head and told him not to, he continued to walk until he had returned to the inside of the fort. He closed the gate behind him and locked it.

He stepped on something in the snow. He stopped and lowered himself to dig.

After some probing under the freezing powder, he found something and then another something. He brought his hands out and found that he was holding Buchanan's pistols.

He frowned.

"He'd never let these things out of his sight. I've seen him polishing these until they could shine in the dark." Abraham thought.

A pit had begun to grow in his chest. As angry as he had been at Buchanan for his quiet dismissal, and refusal to help, he was worried now.

Something had rattled the man, rattled him bad. Whatever it was that could rattle a man like Buchanan, it was 'something awful' indeed.

Abraham dusted the snow from the pistols and carried them to the cabin.

When he entered, he saw Buchanan sleeping on the bed. Caleb slept awkwardly next to him, his mouth yawning open in a deep, and still slightly drunk slumber.

Abraham allowed himself to smile a little bit. A wise and knowing smile, that considered the fiery hangover that awaited the boy when he woke. He placed Buchanan's pistols on a shelf and sighed.

He looked to the table and then to a shelf near it. His journal sat upon it.

He walked toward it and picked it up. He leafed through it, and nodded to himself.

He had always enjoyed journaling. Sometimes, vomiting out your thoughts onto a page and reading through it later, brought insight. Insight and wisdom that could be wrung from the thoughts of a man, reexamined at a later time. Hindsight was 20/20, but unfortunately, unhelpful.

But, a journal could sometimes get a man as close to precognition as the world of reality would allow.

Abraham sat, fetched ink and quill and began to write. What he didn't know however, was that just across the room from him, a battle was being fought.

When the unknown and sinister forces had broadcasted from the forest, and into Buchanan's mind, it hadn't *only* been broadcasting. It had been digging, tilling... cultivating.

It had planted a seed. A parasitic worm of thought, stuffed into the deepest recesses of Buchanan's mind. That worm now dug and burrowed. It feasted and multiplied. It rifled through the files marked; "**PAINFUL**" and dined upon them. It swallowed traumatic memories, and shit paranoia and terror.

Buchanan found himself as a boy, so many years ago now. He couldn't have been a day over ten. He and his younger brother Grant, had spent several weeks constructing a raft.

Their school teacher had regaled them a month prior, with stories of backwoods adventures. Tales of unknown lands, navigated by men of brave heart.

There was a lake a couple miles from their family homestead. He and his younger brother, only eight himself, had walked there many times now. After they had finished their respective chores, they would trek out to the lake, and to their secretly hidden raft.

They had pilfered rope and twine from their Father's supplies here and there, to fasten together the small logs. The logs, they had found near the lake, and the forest around it.

But today... today was the day they would set sail on their maiden-voyage.

They had woken up early. Had rushed through their chores, and had made the walk to the lake.

He and Grant had hauled the raft from its hiding place, and set it at the water's edge.

Buchanan found a long piece of timber that would serve as their push rod. Grant awaited eagerly at the raft's starboard as his brother returned. Moments later, they were pushing off to navigate the treacherous unknown, of the calm, placid lake.

"Injuns at the bank!" Grant had shouted.

"I'll get 'em!" Buchanan had replied, passing the push rod to Grant. He raised his fingers that were molded into the shapes of guns, and fired at the imaginary Indians. The Indians shouted war-cries and shot back arrows at their craft from the bank.

"Pow! You got 'em!" Grant had yelled back in celebration.

And so the day had passed beautifully. This fine summer day, that was gradually winding to a close. Orange glowed along the horizon, shimmering off of the water's surface.

With the threat of imaginary Indians and pirates now eliminated, it was time to relax. The boys laid on their backs, staring up at the auburn-pink sky from the bobbing raft. Buchanan dipped his toes in the water and Grant hummed a tune at his side.

"Why don't Daddy like me Johnny?" Grant had said, breaking the peace.

Buchanan turned, propping himself up on his elbow. "What're you talking about?"

Grant shrugged. "He don't like me the way he does you. He won't even let me come hunting."

Buchanan thought for a moment, trying to figure out how best to respond with the limited understanding of a ten year old.

"He likes you fine." He'd reassured his brother. "I guess he just don't want you to grow up too fast."

"Why would he want that?" Grant had inquired. "I can help too."

"I know that." Buchanan said. "He knows that too. It's just... I get the sense that being a kid is the best time of your life. As funny as that sounds Grant."

Grant raised his shoulders meekly.

"I know he likes you fine. Because, he wants you to stay in that good part for long as you can."

After a moment, Grant sighed. "I guess so. Just wishin' he'd let me come with you. It's boring, hanging around Mama all by myself."

"Soon enough I'd say." Buchanan said and stood. He stretched and waved his arms around. "Well..." He said through a yawn. "I reckon we better get back. It'll be both our hides if we're late for supper."

Horribly then, Buchanan had misstepped. He stumbled and caught his footing on the least sturdy part of the raft. The previously tranquil craft was suddenly thrust upward and vertical.

Buchanan fell down and into the chilly lake. Grant was not so lucky. He was thrust up and out as the raft climbed upward.

Buchanan came up with a gasp of air, and terribly, just in time to see what happened next.

Grant came out of the water that he had been thrown into, just as the raft teetered from its heavenward stance. It fell up and over and came bearing down at Grant.

"Look out!" Buchanan had shouted.

But it was of no use. The lashed timbers of the raft came crashing down all at once on top of Grant's head. The weight of the soaked lumber cracked the poor boy's skull with a powerful blow. It hadn't killed the boy, but it immediately knocked him unconscious.

Grant had gone face down, pinned under the floor of the raft.

Buchanan had swam to him and had pushed the raft aside. He had cradled his brother's bleeding head in his hands and tried to wake him.

He had tried. Oh, how he had tried to swim to shore. But alas, he was not strong enough. Try as he might to keep the boy's head above water, he had not been successful.

When they were almost twenty feet from the shore, Grant had begun to sink.

"Grant!" Buchanan cried, choking and coughing on water. "Wake up! Wake up Grant!"

It had finally become too much. His arms quivered and shook. Buchanan had grown weary, had sucked down water and was struggling to swim. His mind instinctively loosened its grip on the anchor that was dragging it down.

Buchanan fought it, but it didn't last long. He watched as his grip laxed and Grant was let go. The unconscious boy slipped fully below the surface, and began to sink.

Slowly and painfully, he had watched his brother disappear into the black darkness of the depths below.

Coughing and sputtering on the shore, Buchanan had cried, had sobbed. He cried to the heavens and prayed until his voice hurt to bring his brother back.

But it was of no use.

His panicked parents had found him hours later, and his brother would never again return from the depths of his murky tomb.

Buchanan had awoken then, or at least he thought he had. At his side, instead of Caleb on the bed, was now Grant.

His long dead brother stared at him with vacant and hollow sockets where his eyes had been. Filthy lake water spilled from his mouth, as he grinned at his big brother.

Buchanan screamed in equal parts disgust and terror. He tried to stand and run, but Grant grasped his throat.

Strong, so strong this long dead, little boy was. Grant stared at him through those hollow voids in his face, and gazed at the brother who fought to get away.

"Listen to me." Grant had bubbled out. His voice was muffled and gurgling under the gray water that leaked constantly from his mouth. "You did the right thing."

These unexpected words slowed Buchanan, he stopped struggling and looked at his brother. He was hard to look at, but the hollow sockets hypnotized him and held him firm.

"What?" Buchanan meekly managed to say.

The boy grinned. "You did the right thing. You let me go. I was weak and I died. You were strong and you survived."

Buchanan shook his head. The ghost boy tightened his grip around his throat and he felt pressure building under his eyeballs.

"Listen to me!" Grant hissed. "You have forgotten what has allowed you to live so long. You are strong. You did not survive by being lashed to the weak."

Buchanan fought against the icy grip of the small hand. It was no use. A moment later, he met his brother's hollow gaze. He nodded.

"I am strong."

Grant grinned. "You can do what must be done. No matter what it is."

Buchanan stared at him, he nodded again. "I can do grisly things to survive."

Grant nodded this time. "You are a survivor. You will always survive."

Buchanan agreed.

"So you will do what must be done? No matter the cost? Even if it comes to killing the weak that drag you down?" The ghost boy asked.

Buchanan's transfixed gaze began to waiver. "I can't."

The boy frowned, but then grew back his grin. "You will. I see into all that you are. You will do anything to survive."

Buchanan awoke, gasping for air and murmuring confused words. He looked around.

Everything was as it should be. Caleb slept at his side and had begun to stir a little.

Abraham looked up at him from writing in his journal. He appeared worried, and looked sincerely into Buchanan's eyes. "You alright?" He asked.

Buchanan cleared his throat and swallowed. "Yeah. Just a nightmare."

Abraham looked inquisitively at him for a few more seconds and then nodded, going back to his writing.

"How long was I out?" Buchanan asked, rubbing his eyes.

Abraham shrugged. "Since you stormed off? Hour or two. You left your pistols in the snow. I put them on the shelf for you."

Buchanan raised his eyebrows as he thought of this. So much of what Abraham was saying was foreign to him.

"Stormed off?"

He supposed he had. But that recent memory seemed far away now, all scrambled. He looked to the shelf and there were his guns, just as Abraham had said.

"You were going out..." Buchanan said thoughtfully, trying to remember what had happened only a couple of hours ago. "Did... Did you find anything?"

Abraham sighed. "As a matter of fact, I did. Tracks. Tracks unlike any animal known. I followed them for a while and then they just disappeared."

Buchanan thought for a moment, two parts of his brain at war with each other. The thought that he spoke was not his own, but one pushed into his mind like a letter through a slot.

"A lot of this country is unknown. There are pockets of untamed and unexplored wilderness all over. There are bound to be things unknown." Buchanan's voice said it, but his own mind hadn't made him.

Abraham looked up, he considered this quietly to himself. "I suppose. But whatever these things are, they are lethal and large numbered. If we can't leave, and we can't hunt for food, we'll have to kill them."

Another thought pushed its way out of Buchanan's mouth. "They've never bothered us during the day, and we've never seen any sign of them til last night. Maybe they're nocturnal."

Abraham thought on this, nodding. "That's a good point. I hadn't considered that." He thought for another moment. "What do you think we should do then?"

Buchanan shrugged. All at once it felt like whatever had held the steering wheel of his brain, had just let go. He was back in control for the moment. Whatever had been driving a moment before, had steered in its desired direction and no longer needed to guide, for now.

"Well I suppose we do as we've been doing." Buchanan said after a moment. "Hunt during the day and be back before sundown. Until we can find a better plan."

Abraham frowned, he didn't like it. "I suppose that's the best idea at the moment. But the nocturnal thought is just that; a thought. We might have just been getting lucky until now."

"It's either that, or sit here til we starve." Buchanan replied.

Before Abraham could reply to this, Caleb had begun to wake.

He groaned and clutched at the wrapped bandages on his head. "God almighty." He sighed out as he got to his feet. "My head is screaming."

Buchanan laughed a little too hard for Abraham's comfort and slapped Caleb hard on the back. "It's only your first time. They'll get worse the older you get." He said with a bear-like paw on the boy's shoulder.

Caleb groaned and shook his head. "I don't think I'll ever partake again."

Buchanan laughed again, a laugh that just seemed... off. "That's what they all say. Then they're back in the saloon again before supper." Buchanan said with another chuckle.

Caleb suddenly bolted to his feet, sprinted to the door and threw it open. He fell to his knees and vomited violently in the snow.

After he had finished and wiped his mouth, he walked back in. He sat at the table next to Abraham. "What's the plan today?"

Buchanan began to speak up. "Well last night..."

Abraham silenced him with a fiery gaze.

Buchanan took notice and quieted.

"Just as expected." A foreign voice echoed in his head.

"Well last night has got us all fatigued..." Buchanan continued. "Let's take it easy today and resume plans tomorrow." He looked at Abraham. "Wouldn't you agree Mr. Mercer?"

Abraham looked back at him for a moment. Though he couldn't exactly pinpoint what was wrong, there was the slightest trepidation that something was off. When he could not narrow it down enough to put a finger on, he replied. "Yes. Let's take it easy today. Rest up after our foolhardiness."

"Fine by me." Caleb had said as he'd retreated; tail between his legs to the bed. Moments later, he was burrowed under the covers, shivering and groaning.

Buchanan stood and walked toward the door. "I will join you in a moment. I'd like some fresh air."

Abraham had shot a glance at the man that went unnoticed as he left. Suspicions were rising but he couldn't figure out why.

Buchanan simply disappeared out into the courtyard as the door creaked shut behind him.

Stealing glances out of the door occasionally in curiosity, Abraham had returned to journaling.

Nothing had been visibly out of the ordinary. Buchanan had first been walking the perimeter of the fort, occasionally peering out between the slats. He had smoked and hacked badly afterward, as he always did. Now, he was chopping wood for the stove. Abraham, satisfied for the moment, returned to his journal and the page he was writing.

Much has transpired since my last entry. Caleb has recovered well and joined us last night in an impromptu celebration.

Celebration...Ha.

For what? Celebration that we are still alive? Celebration that we were not among our comrades when an outlaw party gunned them down?

What is there to celebrate?

We have no direction, no heading.

Even if we do survive the rest of this winter, what will we do then? Find a town and try to root in?

Complete the journey Clanton and Jacobs set us on?

But to what end, to what purpose?

I will have to take from Laura's legacy and trust in God as she would. For I do not have any semblance of direction any longer.

Abraham continued for a while. Detailing the events of the attack the night prior, as best as he could from what he remembered. He closed the book and rubbed his neck.

He laid his head down on the table. He didn't want to sleep, he just wanted to rest his eyes for a moment. Or so he had told himself. Because a moment later, he was snoring and far away.

Outside, Buchanan was chopping wood still.

Log after log he split.

The others felt horrible. The others were trembling with the effects of a terrible hangover. But Buchanan? Buchanan felt strong. He felt good, for reasons he didn't understand. He had energy and felt well.

He chopped.

He placed another wobbling log onto the chopping block and raised the ax high. Just as he had begun to bring it down, his vision flashed.

He was no longer swinging an ax at a log. He was swinging it at Abraham's neck.

Abraham looked up at him from the log that he laid upon. His eyes stared pleadingly at Buchanan as the ax came down further.

Buchanan jumped. He changed the course of the ax mid swing, and nearly split his foot instead of the wood. He looked up again, Abraham was gone.

The log was just a log again.

He held the ax loosely in his hand and stared at the wood. He waited for it to transform back into one of his comrades.

But it didn't.

He started swinging again.

Chapter 12

Naked. He walked naked, along the shore.

Though he could see his breath, he wasn't cold.

In fact, he realized he couldn't feel anything when he really thought about it. The snow that his bare feet walked upon offered no sensation, in fact, not even the pressure against the ground could be felt.

He turned out, toward the lake.

Across the shimmering surface of black water, was a rowboat. A rowboat with a ghostly lantern at its bow.

The light that beamed from the lantern was incredibly intense. It hurt his eyes to look at, it was the only thing he could feel.

He could not make out the driver of the boat through the brilliance of the glimmering beam. But, he could, however, see Caleb at its stern.

Caleb was tied tightly in ropes and chains, he struggled against them. His mouth was gagged and he tried to call out to the man on the shore. His eyes were wide, bulging. He pleaded with those watery and bulbous eyes, to the man on the beach that watched him back.

Abraham shouted back to Caleb on the boat. But even though his own mouth wasn't gagged, his voice made no sound.

He was reduced to a naked being with no voice. A man without sense, shouting into the void.

Abraham shot up in his bedroll. He patted his chest and body. He was clothed and back in reality.

The cabin was empty.

Spurred with panic at this realization, he jumped to his feet and burst out the door. His fear was quieted quickly though, as outside he found Buchanan and Caleb.

They weren't gone. They weren't rowing a ghostly boat in a nonexistent lake.

Caleb was sitting at the outside campfire, poking at the coals with a stick and looking bored. Buchanan chopped wood and stacked it high in a very large pile against the fence.

All was right for the moment. Everything looked ordinary at the surface.

Abraham breathed a sigh of relief quietly to himself. They could make it. They could navigate these murky and treacherous waters yet. Something in him just knew it and reassured him.

They would simply do as they had decided. Hunt during the day and hunker down at night. Tough it out until Spring when they could make a run for it. They could make it through.

All they had to do was stick to the plan.

So they had, unfortunately.

Eight days had passed. They had hunted during the day as planned but had not gotten anything. They hadn't seen so much as the odd squirrel in all eight days.

It was as if every beast and creature of the wood had unanimously agreed to vacate. To seek out greener pastures and leave these dwindling men behind.

Each day, Abraham and Buchanan had ventured out into the woods and had come home empty handed.

Caleb had wanted to come of course, but at Abraham's insistence had remained behind.

"Not until you've fully recovered." He had said.

This had been good and well intentioned advice at first, as Caleb was still very weak. He could scarcely walk a lap in the courtyard end to end, without coming back winded.

But now, he had grown back strong. He was still not 100% but getting close. He was building himself back piece by piece and his patience with Abraham's protectiveness was wearing thin.

But, for the eight days he had obeyed and had waited behind. He had shut the gate behind the two departing men. He had stayed behind like the lame foal that he felt like.

Out in the woods, Abraham admittedly was the only one really hunting.

Buchanan was off, his head was seemingly in the clouds, and it didn't feel like he was out here for any other reason than ceremony.

He would stop suddenly and for long moments, staring off into nothing. He would come to his senses a minute later and look afraid, lost.

But whenever Abraham would question him about it, he would simply say that he was tired and hungry.

They were.

They were all very hungry. The stowed rations that they had begun to cut into more and more, were all but gone.

Their heads burned with migraines and their muscles ached after days without rest and fuel. Tensions were high and felt as if they could pop at any moment.

Now, on the morning of the ninth day, this seeping boil would begin to rupture.

Abraham awoke like he had for too long, hungry and weak. He rose from his uncomfortable spot on the floor, his bedroll unkempt and worn.

When they had first gotten here, so long ago now, he had volunteered to have the floor. Caleb would have a spot in the bed by default, given his condition. The other spot was given to Buchanan who was the elder.

Of course, they could have slept in other cabins, where they could all have had their own beds.

But on nights where the wind howled and beat against this hollow sentry in the wood, it was nice not to be alone.

Aside from the other obvious reason; of sticking together in case of any unexpected trouble. It really was the ominous atmosphere of this place that drove them all together when the sun went down.

Abraham stood, stretching his sore bones and tired muscles. He looked at the table.

On a section of fabric, there were a small assortment of crumbs; leftovers from the hard tack biscuits the night before. He licked his finger and rolled it over the pitiful remains. He brought the fingertip to his mouth and savored the salt and dry tack, he was so goddamn hungry.

He went to the bed and rounded it to the far side where Buchanan snored. He shook the old man's shoulder and sleepily muttered: "Buchanan."

No response was given from the sleeping man.

Growing slightly angry, and already short from the growling of his stomach, Abraham shook him harder. "Buchanan!" He shouted.

Buchanan didn't stir, but Caleb did. He sat up in the bed and looked around.

"What is it?" He asked.

Abraham shook his head. "Dammit. Another battle with Caleb." He thought.

"Nothing." He said to the boy. "Go back to sleep."

"Are you going out hunting?" Caleb asked eagerly. "Let me go this time! Think back to the journey's start, I snared the first game of the trip!"

Abraham nodded, feigning agreement. He had heard this pitch every morning for the last week and he knew every angle of it. Still, it was hard every time. The thought of those smoking rabbits on the spit all that time ago, brought moisture to his tongue.

But, he just couldn't do it. He had wanted to bring Caleb many times now, but he couldn't follow through.

The boy had nearly died on his watch already, and that was before they had witnessed the beasts of hell tear apart an outlaw raiding party.

These woods were simply too dangerous to willingly bring the kid into. Caleb was the last remaining remnant of his wife. The last person alive that had ever actually known her.

Clanton and crew were dead, getting picked clean by the buzzards by now, and Buchanan hadn't ever said more than four words to her.

No, Caleb was the last living person, the last living piece that knew Laura Mercer. The last person he could converse with about her, could reminisce about her, and keep her alive in the smallest sense of the word.

As selfish as it was and as much as he hated himself for it, he could not risk Caleb.

Before Abraham could respond to the pleading boy, Buchanan woke up yelling.

Yelling? No, howling.

He thrashed this way and that, looking wildly around the room before the world of reality came back to him.

Caleb and Abraham had jumped back, frightened by the outburst. They now eyed him curiously.

"Mr. Buchanan?" Caleb said softly. "You alright sir?"

Buchanan looked scared, he looked tired and alone.

He looked like a bear cub that had lost its mother. A timid and tired creature roaming the wilderness with its anchor and guide ripped away from it.

A vulnerable and naked pup, navigating The Valley of the Shadow of Death, and fearing all the evil within.

He spoke up almost a minute later. He was slow, as if he didn't know where he was but had started to remember.

"Nightmare. My apologies." He said to the boy after he had understood him.

"Let's go." Abraham said. "We need to hunt."

Buchanan blinked and shed another layer of his shell of incoherence. "Yes. Of course." He replied a moment later.

Buchanan had gotten ready painfully slow, a fact that grew Abraham's irritable temper even more.

Caleb had gotten ready too, not prepared to give up his request to be of use.

Finally, Abraham had led the man out of the door and toward the gate. Caleb was bringing up the rear and ready to follow them.

As the gate swung open, as it had every morning now for nine days, Buchanan halted mid-step. He was standing now, one foot in and one foot out of the fort.

Something had frozen him in place, and he looked as if he had just been socked in the gut by a cannonball.

The broadcast, the voices that had been silent for all the days prior, had suddenly crackled back into life.

The broadcasting and the seed were now working in tandem. They had grown to know this mind as well as they'd known every knot, in every tree of the woods. He was easy now to control, to persuade.

What had started as whispers, now were as clear as day with commands.

The instructions that had just blasted into Buchanan's mind with the force of a freight train, were this:

"Not today. Today you will not leave."

"I cannot." Buchanan said stiffly.

Abraham looked at him with confusion, his irritation growing into anger. "What? We don't have time for this Buchanan, let's go."

Abraham was confused, but had gradually noticed the fragile layers of Buchanan's brain begin to snap.

The man had shrunk into a former shell of himself. Day by day, he had gone more and more mad. As infuriating as it was, Buchanan's eyes could not be argued with. His mind was made up.

Plain and simple, this man would not be leaving this place today.

Caleb stood back in the courtyard, watching the scene play out. He didn't care what the matter was with Buchanan, be it a case of the sniffles or full blown cholera. He didn't care especially, if it meant that he would finally be able to get out of the fort for once. He was going stir crazy and needed a change of scenery.

Abraham awaited a response from the silent, stubborn man. "Hello?" He called to Buchanan's distant eyes.

"You are afraid. You are so very afraid." The Broadcast spoke.

"No. I cannot. Not today." Buchanan said sheepishly, and began to walk back inside.

Abraham shook his head and lowered it.

"I'll go!" Caleb interjected excitedly. "Buchanan can rest up and I'll take his watch."

"No." Abraham said authoritatively. "Not yet."

Caleb's patience at these words, had finally met the end of its rope. "Goddammit Abraham! I'm about to go mad as Buchanan!"

Buchanan didn't react, didn't even notice these words. He was far away.

Caleb continued with his angry shouting. "If you ain't gonna use me, gonna have me sitting around here like some damn barn cat manning the fort... Well then, I might as well have stayed with Clanton!"

Buchanan's head sprang into life and thought again.

"Speak what you know." His mind broadcasted.

"If you'd have stayed with Clanton, you'd be as dead as he is." Buchanan said frankly.

Caleb's jaw dropped as he heard these words, and he spun around to look at Buchanan.

Abraham winced and scowled simultaneously.

Caleb spun back to Abraham. "Is that true?"

Abraham didn't answer.

"Goddammit! Is that true?!" Caleb yelled, tears forming in his eyes.

"Yes." Abraham sighed.

"Why didn't you tell me?" He demanded.

Abraham rubbed his eyes in exhaustion, as he thought of what to say. "I didn't want to worry you. Didn't want you to give up hope."

"I ain't no schoolboy Abraham! What I can and can't handle ain't for you to decide." Caleb shouted. Anger, brought on by betrayal and the incessant hunger, burned hot and strong. "You ain't my Goddamn father. You don't get to decide what's best for me. I'm my own man and you need to know that!"

Caleb stormed off, back to the cabin. The notion of the hunting trip long forgotten. He was boiling with this perceived insult to his maturity and manhood. Surprisingly quick, he had disappeared back into the cabin and slammed the door.

Buchanan turned to Abraham who was still staring at the cabin, eyes angry, but also hurt.

"He'll cool off." Buchanan offered. "I just can't do it today Mr. Mercer. I wish you luck."

Before Abraham could answer, Buchanan had bundled his coat tightly around himself and was walking back up to the cabin to join Caleb.

Still hot with anger and stinging with pain, Abraham gritted his teeth, shook his head, and walked away from the fort to the woods.

He was alone and felt nearly naked.

Chapter 13

Buchanan split a log. The almost rhythmic motions of it were the only thing that could bring him small moments of clarity.

He had felt so hazy for the last week. Reality and dreams blended together so seamlessly, that it made his head spin.

For some reason, he had gravitated toward the chopping of firewood. Maybe, given something to focus on, he could have a moment's coherence. A moment to try and sort through the haphazard files of his brain, and put them into two separate bins; real and not real.

THUNK!

He split another log and things became a little more clear. The boy was in the cabin, that was real. The boy was in the cabin and was upset.

Upset? Why?

He needed to be consoled. No, not consoled. Just needed company.

Buchanan set down the ax, and began to walk away.

Then, the seed spoke up again, freezing him.

Though the old bounty hunter once known as John Buchanan, was fighting, fighting with every inch of his life, no one would know it by looking at him.

The man looked drunk, paralyzed and catatonic. He stood, hovering in a liminal space between this world and something else.

But in his head, the battle of all battles was raging.

A moment later, John Buchanan had color return to his eyes. He nodded slightly and began to walk.

Inside the cabin, Caleb sat on the bed. The kid fiddled with his hands and obviously was working something over and over in his head. He looked up briefly when Buchanan entered, but resigned himself to the invisible knot his hands were tying.

Buchanan lumbered to the bed and sat down next to the boy. His gaze was far off and deep in thought. When he decided that the boy wasn't going to break the silence, he did.

"What's twisting your mind boy?" He asked.

Caleb swallowed. "Is it that plain?" He said with a weak laugh. "I've done something Mr. Buchanan. Something I sure do want off my chest."

Buchanan nodded slowly. "I know the look. Unload my boy."

Caleb tightened his lips and furrowed his brow. He was clearly battling with something he desperately wanted to speak out loud, but could not figure out how.

"I..." Caleb began, but quickly silenced again. He swallowed with a gulp. "If'n, If'n we don't make it out of here. Out of this place. I don't want to die weighted down with sin."

Buchanan looked at him with a gaze of slight interest. He nodded for the kid to continue.

"Back with Clanton and all them. When things was real rough. Was real bad... I snared a big ole rabbit." Caleb stopped, drawing in a few snot-gagged sniffles. "I was so damn hungry... So hungry. I hid it from the others. I scarfed it down so greedily that Judas would even blink. I ate it up, without a care for anyone else. And I slept... I slept so good with that belly full of greed."

Buchanan didn't respond after Caleb had entered these final words into consideration. He simply sat, absently thinking.

Caleb watched Buchanan, awaiting something, any sort of response. He had just confessed his most regretted misdeed and was met with silence.

He threw something else into the ring, anything to break this godforsaken silence.

"I ain't never been this hungry Mr. Buchanan. Not even then." Caleb said, his eyes watchful on Buchanan's expression.

"I have." Buchanan said absently and suddenly.

Caleb nodded in a gesture of listening, awaiting the next confession in this bleak sermon.

"Famine brought on by drought." Buchanan said. He looked to Caleb as he spoke this, his eyes met those of the young boy, and a small, warm twinge of compassion was brought into his heart. He began to speak more friendly, more engaging.

"If these army boys had had any lick of sense, they'd have been breeding rabbits." Buchanan said in an open-ended way. "The least they could have done as a thanks, for us watching over their place and all."

Caleb thought for a moment before he engaged. "Rabbits?" He asked, curiously.

"Indeed." Buchanan said with a sniff. "Rabbits would put a whore to shame on her busiest night. Always screwing, always breeding."

Caleb laughed a little at the analogy as Buchanan continued.

"If done correctly, breeding rabbits can yield a never-ending supply of meat. If'n you've got the stomach for it." Buchanan relayed.

"I don't mind rabbit." Caleb said with a raised brow. "Doesn't sound so bad to me."

Buchanan nodded with a pained grin. "I do." He coughed and cleared his throat. "This little expedition is the first time I've eaten rabbit in over twenty years."

Caleb looked to him, awaiting the story that was surely to come.

Buchanan thought visibly. He dredged a thought that was long dormant and stored on the highest shelves of his mind.

"I was once in this real shit-hole of a saloon. Up in the mountains real high, not too unlike this place. About all they had to offer to eat was rabbit in one way or another." He sniffed again. "Rabbit stew, rabbit leg, rabbit and beans." Buchanan spoke as if he were describing the contents of an outhouse, his face was wrinkled and disgusted.

"All of that sounds quite agreeable to me." Caleb said, still watchful of the old man's expression.

"I'm sure it does." Buchanan spoke. "But not to me. I'd rather eat the north-end of a south-bound mule, given the chance."

Caleb moved to laugh, but it didn't come. He simply agreed. "I would most likely partake as well." He offered shyly.

"Any man would if they were thrust into our shoes." Buchanan replied. He swallowed back the drool that had formed in his mouth. Drool that was brought from the notion of eating the fried ass of a mangy old mule. A truly pitiful sight their lot was.

Several moments of silence followed, silence that Buchanan broke after some more searching of the high shelves of his mind.

"Anyhow." Buchanan continued. "I asked the proprietor of this saloon once about the menu. I asked him; "How come everything has at least a bite of rabbit in it?" Well, this cheery, old-chinaman type... He told me what I just told you. How a couple rabbits can be a nearly endless supply of meat." Buchanan swallowed back some vile spit and forced himself into the deeper layers of the memory. "Then after I had called bullshit and had laughed at his explanation, he led me to the rabbit pen."

Caleb watched as a light flashed almost visibly behind Buchanan's eyes.

"When I seen what lay in that stinking, old straw filled shed... I about tossed my guts. About threw up a week's worth of rabbit stew onto the ground."

Caleb, heavily invested in this tale now, prodded Buchanan for more. "How come?" He asked insistently.

Buchanan took a deep breath in, searching for the words that would describe the filthy scene he had witnessed that day, so long ago.

"The... Mother of the brood had been bred a lot. I mean a good Goddamn lot. She'd been bred so long that her teats sagged and dragged against the ground when she moved. She looked at me, I know it. She looked right at me and begged the man that stared at her to kill her, to bring upon her mercy."

"Jesus." Caleb breathed.

"She'd been bred so long that the newest members of her brood weren't right. The *youngins* weren't right. Some were missing eyes, others legs. Some were simply blind, wriggling masses of fur upon the ground. And there they would stay. Until that old chinaman plucked them from their unseeing, and unhearing tomb to be added to the stew." Buchanan sniffed and cleared his throat again. He was quiet for several moments longer before finishing. "I never ate rabbit again after that. Not til them two you snared when we first set off."

Caleb was quiet for a long time now. There were many mental images and tastes in his mouth to work through. When he had cleared all that swirled in his head, all he could say was; "Well I have at least lost my appetite for the time being."

Buchanan nodded. "Then the tale has had the desired effect. Rest up boy. While you can." Buchanan stood and left, leaving Caleb behind to dwell in the afterthought of these musings. The philosophies and tales of the well-traveled; John Buchanan.

Caleb shivered, wrapped himself in the heavy quilt of the bed, and allowed himself to doze.

Deep in the woods now, Abraham walked with a rifle in his hands. He stopped and crouched every now and then, trying his best to find some tracks. It was growing late, but he would not head back until it was dark enough that he couldn't see.

He had to come up with something, anything. He imagined coming back with a puny chipmunk in his pocket, or a songbird. He laughed to himself weakly at this thought. The obliterated, miniscule meat would be bleeding in his pocket, and absorbing all the flavors of fabric in his coat or pants.

Though, even if he did bag some small rodent or bird, he didn't know for certain if he'd even make it back with what was left of it. He felt his body might take control at the sight of fresh meat, and he would devour it all; fur, or feathers, and beak all the same.

The haze of encroaching starvation stung at his head then. He was hit with a throbbing and angry headache and grew woozy. He found a boulder that wasn't completely buried under the snow, and sat down.

He just needed to rest for a moment or else he would pass out entirely.

Back in the cabin at Fort Preston, Buchanan stood over the slumbering Caleb. He stared down at the boy who slept peacefully under the heavy quilt.

He looked at the boy's cheeks, noticing that they had finally regained their color. He stared at the clean bandages atop his head, the wraps that were almost not needed now.

But then, in a blink, Caleb was gone.

Under the blankets now, was instead a lamb. A tiny and meek creature that slept quietly. Buchanan admired the petite and fluffy creature. A baby, just starting to grow its wool for the first time.

His heart warmed slightly at the sight of the small, and contently resting creature. Its nose twitched slightly in its slumber, and it rolled over a little to find a more comfortable position.

Buchanan leaned down to pet the little lamb and admire it. But as he stroked its head, the infant stirred and looked at him. The lamb looked at him blankly, unafraid and not curious.

Buchanan smiled, and removed the covers to pick the animal up and cradle it. When the lower half of the lamb was revealed though, he recoiled in shock.

Each of the infant's legs had been savagely broken. The fractures were abrupt and brutal. The little creature's legs were each bent, at sharp, ninety-degree angles. Bones stuck out from the wrinkly new skin, and blood wept from below the jagged and protruding bones.

The lamb looked at him and bleated loudly, high pitched and horrible. The pitiful cries were so piercingly loud, that Buchanan gripped his ears in pain. He felt the deafening sound crackling against his eardrums, the sound that threatened to rupture them.

It cried at him, audibly in so much pain. It squeaked and whined like a puppy limping on a broken paw.

Buchanan begged with the sound, that it should finally cease. But, it continued, undeterred. It bleated and shrieked at the man who stood above it.

The saddening and agonized cries of the baby, forced Buchanan to look down at it again.

He didn't want to look, didn't want to see it again. But, something beyond his control pulled his gaze down.

The lamb looked at him blankly, though its cries were as hysterical as ever. It stared into his eyes. It pleaded with him, it begged him to depart it from this misery.

Buchanan's eyes watered at the stabbing pain from the helpless cries. He wanted to help. He wanted to take the pain away from the sobbing creature.

Then, the lamb was gone, but the bed wasn't empty. The resident of the cot didn't vanish, it only changed.

It was the mother of the rabbit brood, teats sagging and bloody.

It was Grant, sinking below the surface and dragging him down.

It was his baby brother, his father's hand over its mouth.

"I will release you." He breathed distantly. "I will take away the pain."

This was the last thing he said before placing his hands around Caleb's throat.

Abraham sat on the boulder in the clearing, catching his breath. His head pounded in his ears and his chest heaved. His legs and arms burned with the pleas of the muscles within. They begged him to stop, to rest. He was broken, hopeless and lost.

But just then, unbelievably, and terribly sudden, the most beautiful sight in the world caught his gaze.

A deer was crossing the clearing about fifty yards away from him.

A deer, a real deer.

This was not the piteous fawn they had dined upon more than a week ago. This was a buck, antlers gone at this time of the year, but large and full of meat. The answer to the most pressing of their immediate problems, had stumbled out in front of him, ready to be partaken of.

Trying his best to steady his excited and trembling hands, Abraham slowly raised the rifle and brought the deer into his sights. He breathed and began to put pressure onto the trigger. He could very nearly taste the fatty venison under the fine fur of the buck's side. Fatty, plump meat that would crackle on the fire and tickle his nose with its aroma.

The firing pin was an instant away from dropping. An instant away from igniting the gunpowder, and propelling its lead doom toward the hapless animal.

But, either fate or something more deliberate, had much different plans for this hunter and his comrades.

A crack behind him.

A large and deliberate crack of a twig, from something sneaking up on him. The timeframe of only one-second stretched into slow motion and Abraham was afraid.

The fine hairs of his neck abruptly stood at attention. The parcel of testicles between his legs shriveled up into a tight, fleshy walnut.

The indescribable human instinct that fires fast and hot. The undeniable feeling that something is horribly, horribly wrong.

Survival instinct took the wheel.

Abraham whirled around from the deer and brought his gun to whatever was closing in.

That was when he was brought face to face with The Rogue.

There he was, as he had always been. Painted pale white and an animalistic fury behind his eyes. He was fast and cunning.

He moved over the snow with ease, lightning quick and incredibly agile. He was sprinting full speed and no more than five feet away now.

Abraham pulled the trigger, right as The Rogue swatted away the barrel of the rifle with his tomahawk. The shot went off into the air, and Abraham was tackled to the ground.

Caleb fought hard against the leathery and icy hands that closed around his throat.

He had been dreaming well a moment before. Now suddenly, he had been ripped out, awoken in pain and confusion.

Buchanan was straddling him now, his eyes staring into Caleb's with nothing behind them. His gaze was hollow and far away.

Caleb could feel his eyes bulging and his throat burning. Try as he might, he could not loose the grip that tightened ever more around his windpipe.

His vision blurred and he felt the sensation of his extremities fading away. As a last resort and mostly out of reflex, he brought his knee up hard into Buchanan's groin.

A muted yelp escaped Buchanan's mouth as he loosened his grip. Caleb crunched a knee into Buchanan's balls again and grabbed his wrists, heaving sideways and sending both of them crashing to the floor.

Caleb landed flat on his back and felt the wind escape his lungs. Buchanan toppled over and out, sending the table crashing over. Plates shattered and a kettle clanged against the floor.

Caleb struggled to catch his breath and formulate some sort of plan. He looked toward the woodpile near the stove and crawled toward it. A heavy, knot-filled log was in his sights.

Buchanan was back on him in an instant, hands closing again around his throat.

The brief clarity of non-strangled vision, had allowed Caleb to see something. As Buchanan had wrestled him back down and straddled a leg over his torso, a godsend had glinted against the light of the filtering sun. A knife was tied in a sheath to Buchanan's thigh. He reached for it.

Buchanan grunted, spittle leaking from his bared teeth. He slammed Caleb's head against the floor, rocking his vision and stunning him. Nonetheless, Caleb fought through and grabbed the handle of the knife.

The violence of the scuffle had loosened the tied leather strips that held the knife, and it was loose in its sheath. He withdrew it, and plunged it deep into the thigh that had held it. Caleb felt warmth spurt against his hand, and the smell of iron was heavy in the stale cabin air.

Buchanan howled angrily. His eyes did not change back to normal, they only grew more fierce.

Given a slight opening, Caleb heaved the man off of him and scrambled to his feet.

Buchanan jumped up surprisingly fast, and stood between Caleb and the door. He stood, wavering on his wounded leg and yanked the knife from it. Blood dripped from the shining blade as Buchanan held it and stared into Caleb.

Caleb looked to his side and grabbed the first thing that he saw.

The fire poker from the wood burning stove.

He wished that the fire had been going. Then, the spear might have been glowing orange and fiery hot. He wished for any advantage against this unhinged and bloodthirsty Buchanan.

He swung the fire poker out and away from himself. The metal wooshed loudly through the air with the wild swing.

Buchanan jumped back a little bit, dodging the poker and tightening the grip he held on the bloody knife.

Abraham had been pinned to the ground under The Rogue. He had managed to wrestle away the tomahawk, but was still in a terrible position.

The Indian held a knife in his hand now. A hand that Abraham was holding back tightly by the wrist. The Rogue was bearing down on him with his entire body weight, the razor-sharp knife pointed right at Abraham's heart.

Abraham's arms struggled against the weight of the attacker. His arm muscles began to wiggle, to give out.

The Rogue was expressionless, his eyes cold and unfeeling. But God. He was so strong. The ghostly attacker was unrelenting... and winning.

Just as his grip laxed and the knife slipped downward, Abraham turned slightly to the side.

The knife pierced his flesh, but not his heart. The weapon had plunged into his shoulder instead.

Abraham screamed as the feeling of white-hot fire pierced his shoulder, and stopped on bone. Underneath the muffling layers of muscles and flesh, he thought he almost could hear the screech of metal against his bones.

The Rogue withdrew the knife and raised it, this time intent on its target and the kill.

Abraham drew his leg back and kicked The Rogue hard in the stomach, sending him backward with an audible gasp of air from his mouth. He grabbed a fistful of mud and snow from the base of a tree at his side, and hurled it into The Rogue's face just as he had begun to rush back.

The attacker stumbled backward, blinded by the freezing dirt that stung his eyes.

This brief second of disarmament, allowed Abraham to snatch a large log on the ground and scramble to his feet. He brought the log upward into The Rogue's jaw in a diagonal motion.

The Rogue fell onto his back, flat on the ground. Stunned, but still conscious.

Abraham turned and scrambled across the snow, toward his rifle that laid in the clearing.

The Rogue dove through the air and landed on Abraham's back. The still slightly blinded attacker swung the knife downward and narrowly missed Abraham's head.

Abraham swung his elbow up and into The Rogue's nose, he felt it break and felt warm blood falling onto the back of his neck.

He crawled now, the rifle still in his sights, and he was getting close. Just as his fingers grazed the cold barrel of the rifle, he felt another shot of white-hot, piercing pain.

The Rogue had plunged the knife into his calf muscle. He drew back from the rifle in a spasm of pain and delivered a savage kick to The Rogue's face.

The force of the kick drove The Rogue backward, his grip still tight on the knife. It came out of Abraham's calf sideways, tearing and ripping flesh as it went.

Finally, he had his hands on the rifle. He brought it to his shoulder and aimed, just as The Rogue had gotten to his feet and had begun to charge, knife in hand.

In the quiet and freezing solitude of the forest surrounding Fort Preston, a gunshot rang out.

Buchanan charged Caleb, ducking under another swing of the fire poker and buried the knife into Caleb's side.

The sudden force of pain caused Caleb to drop the fire poker, as Buchanan tackled him to the ground.

Both men clattered to the floor, Buchanan on top of Caleb. The jarring landing caused Buchanan's hand to leave the knife that was still sticking from the boy's ribs. Buchanan's hands were around Caleb's neck again, the knife forgotten.

The boy struggled to breathe, both from the mitts that crushed in on his neck and the punctured lung the knife had provided.

With his last ounce of will, he brought his hand to the knife in his side and forced himself to grab it. He felt the cold metal shift inside him and he nearly passed out. Agonizingly slow, he pulled the serrated knife from between his two ribs.

He could see it now, his next move. The second he could draw the knife out, he would plunge it into this mad man's neck. He would do it with his last ounce of strength, and would vanquish his attacker.

But that didn't happen.

Just as Caleb had the knife about halfway out of himself, Buchanan noticed and slapped his hand against the hilt of the knife. The blade reentered Caleb's side at a new and awkward angle. Caleb screamed and shuddered violently with pain. His last bit of will, gone.

The boy's veins and eyes bulged as he looked up at the attacker. He tried to say something. His lips moved and his tongue wriggled to form a word. But all that came out was gurgling.

A moment later, Buchanan's crushing grip unrelenting, Caleb's throat rattled death and his windpipe collapsed with a soft crunch.

Buchanan heaved himself off of the boy and caught his breath. He wiped hair from his face and clutched at his bleeding leg. He looked down at what he had done.

"A Mercy." He said distantly. "I will always do what must be done."

In the forest, The Rogue lay atop Abraham. Both men were lying still and not moving. Blood seeped out from under both of them and steam wafted up from the bodies of the men.

Then, Abraham stirred. The dead Indian on top of him was heavy, so Goddamn heavy. He had fired straight into The Rogue's face as he had charged, and the back of his head was blasted open. Steam rose from a gaping hole that wafted just below Abraham's nose.

But, The Rogue had not died without incident. Aside from the still weeping knife wounds in his shoulder and leg, he had taken one final blow from the dying sentry. As The Rogue had fallen, the knife still clutched tightly in death, he had pierced Abraham's stomach.

Now, as he sized up the dead weight that pinned him to the freezing earth, he could feel it. If he was going to heave this corpse off of himself, the knife was coming with it.

He lifted with all of his remaining strength, and gradually, The Rogue came up and away from him. Once, on his first attempt, his grip had slipped and The Rogue had fallen again, the knife reinserting itself. His throat spasmed at the sickening feeling of re-penetration and it was several minutes before he would attempt again.

Now, after using every ounce of his remaining strength, he threw the seemingly unkillable sentry off of him and into the snowbank at his side.

Painstakingly, he had stood, and then fallen. He had lost a lot of blood, and was very weak.

At his side, a long and sturdy looking stick lay upon the snow. He clutched it and brought himself to his feet with tongue-biting pain.

One step, then another.

Painfully, he limped along the path back to the fort. One hand clutched to his stomach and the other white-knuckling the walking stick.

He stumbled back toward the way he had come, knowing ultimately in his mind that he would not make it.

Buchanan sat next to the courtyard fire, his eyes far away and in thought. He nibbled nervously at his lip, thinking of what had transpired. He dropped his head violently and vomited onto the ground. He raised his head from between his legs a moment later, and wiped the flecks of sick from his beard.

Wincing as he did, he stood with his hand clasped to a new bandage on his leg. He drew a pistol and walked to the gate, limping every other step.

Sliding the gate to its fully open position, he scanned the woods beyond and awaited Abraham's return, gun in hand.

Minutes passed.

Then ten, then twenty. After thirty had passed, he fumbled the pistol nervously in his grip.

"Goddammit." Buchanan muttered to himself and stepped out beyond the gate. Toward the forest he strode, limping and muttering under his breath.

As he reached the first line of trees, he cocked back the hammer and scanned around, expecting something. He was jumpy, growing more nervous with each step.

"Abraham?!" He called out into the woods.

Nothing.

Buchanan walked a while longer. The sun was setting and the tired orange glinted over everything in its sight. A vitality had started to become active in the forest, sensed only in Buchanan.

The ancient timbers of the pines creaked and cracked as they stretched into life. The wind blustered and howled in sudden gusts. But Buchanan knew better.

The wind was not howling. The forest was breathing, taking its first waking gasps of the night.

"Abraham!" He called again. "Goddammit!"

Abraham limped along with his walking stick. A sudden gust of wind had started and the cold stung his cheeks. His teeth were grinding and his face was scrunched up tightly; the universal expression of someone forcing their way through great pain.

A root, winding like a snake, through rock and earth alike, snagged his foot with its looped grasp. He fell forward, cursing as he did.

His shoulder hit first and the pain was as fresh as ever. He rolled down a shallow embankment and came to a stop at the bottom.

He gasped, catching his breath and spitting snow from his nose and mouth. Groaning, he tried to roll to his side and stand. A shooting pain in his stomach curdled his breath and seized every muscle in motion. He sighed weakly and rolled over to his back again.

"Come on!" Abraham hissed to himself.

With all the sheer force of will, and determined spirit he could muster, he tried to boost himself to stand. Clotting blood gave way with a sickening shift and he relented, collapsing back onto his ass.

"Shit!" He yelled.

Abraham shouted, kicked and cursed with the utter frustration of his predicament. He pounded at the snow with his good arm and carried on, until his voice had grown hoarse and his body had been exhausted.

Not too far away, in these same woods Buchanan's ears perked up at the muffled commotion. Echoing shouts and bellows rebounded off the trees and signaled toward something further down the trail.

Holding his pistol tighter, Buchanan walked in the direction of the sound.

Complete exhaustion had covered Abraham in a lead blanket. His cries had been reduced to tired whispers and gasps of air. "I'm sorry." Was all he managed to mutter to the heavens, before unconsciousness finally took him and silenced his voice for good. He flopped limply onto his back and his head lolled against the freezing ground.

Buchanan walked, ever jumpy and trigger-happy. He extended his pistol out in front of him, following the vacant, hollow eye of the barrel as it searched the trees.

A sound of shuffling behind his back caused him to spin around and fire vaguely in its direction. Smoke wafted from the gun as he stared out into the quiet forest, his shot echoing off into silence. After he had been satisfied that nothing would emerge from the trees he had fired into, he continued walking.

As he rounded a particularly large trunk of a long, felled tree, he saw him.

At the bottom of a shallow embankment lay the unconscious body of Abraham.

"Abraham?" Buchanan floated to the body cautiously.

The sleeping man did not respond. Faint steam rose from his lips, but he did not stir.

"Abraham." He began again, his voice rebounding off every surface of the somber forest. "The boy's dead."

At these words, he jumped back a little. With his finger trembling on the trigger, he watched the unconscious man observantly.

But still, the sleeping man did not stir.

"I killed him." Buchanan said sternly, growing more confident.

Still, the sleeping man did not stir.

Satisfied that Abraham would not spring to life and gun him down at this admission, Buchanan began the descent down the embankment toward the body.

When he had reached him, Buchanan lowered his head to hover, just over Abraham's lips. When he could feel the faintest warmth of a shallow breath, he nodded to himself.

Holstering his pistol, he wrapped his arms around Abraham's limp form and began to heave him onto his shoulder.

Even with his marred leg, so strong he was.

With him alone in this forest, with only an unconscious body, no suspicions were raised. But, if he were to have performed this feat in front of an audience, a man of his stature and age would surely be accused of some form of trickery.

He settled the unconscious man into a comfortable position on his shoulder and began to walk up the embankment. With Abraham's arms and legs swaying lazily against him, he finally crested the top of the hill and began the trek back home.

Buchanan himself felt good, felt the strongest and surest he had felt in a long time. He fancied that in different circumstances, what he was doing would be seen as heroic. Dragging a dying man back from the frozen wilderness and into the warmth of shelter was hardly something in the scope of Buchanan's wheelhouse. It was very fitting that even though he was doing it, it wasn't what it seemed.

Along the trail and frozen tracks that had led from the fort and into the wilderness, Buchanan walked. He continued along, breathing easily despite the weight that he carried.

Dark had begun to grow more and more prevalent, and Buchanan had to squint over the muted glow of the white snow. The moon shimmered eerily downward, muted by the thin wisps of clouds that floated by.

A shriek.

A shriek from one of those things. The terrible shriek of the unknown sounded from somewhere, and it echoed off every section of bark in these godforsaken pines.

Buchanan fell to his knees, defensive and afraid. He pulled Abraham off of his shoulder and into his lap. Inching backward, he came to rest against the base of a tree and tucked both of them in, hiding as best he could.

For a long stretch of crushing silence, they just sat.

They sat, Buchanan consciously feeling the snow beneath his ass melt and soak into his trousers.

Abraham was far away, a fever dream buzzing loudly in his unconscious mind.

Then, he heard it. Subtly at first, and then growing louder and closer. A huffing, a heavy breathing of something massive.

Accompanying these wet, deep breaths, was the heavy sound of enormous footsteps crunching along the snow in long, lumbering strides.

Closer they grew, louder they grew. He felt his neck hairs prickle and rise. The snout of whatever was out there, was zeroing in on the two cowering men at the base of the old pine.

Then, silence.

Absolute and swallowing silence. The force of silence that is aggressive in its present absence. Pounding on the eardrums with the lack of sound.

Out from his side it emerged. A beastly snout slid from the edge of the tree, coming to rest only a few inches from Buchanan's face.

Steam rose from its nostrils as it drank in what it had come to find. Putrid saliva dripped from its teeth and fell upon the snow with viscous consistency.

It was terrifying in its partial absence.

Buchanan could not make out anything, besides the dripping teeth and snout. He could only imagine what creature beyond that they belonged to.

It shrieked again, point blank and inches from his ears. It took all of his willpower to not scream in terror, and the pain that wooshed into his eardrums.

But then, the ghastly snout withdrew and disappeared behind the tree. The massive frame of the unearthly thing lumbered off, with ground-quaking weight. They were left alone and undisturbed.

Buchanan wiped some of the putrid drool that had fallen upon his sleeve and gathered himself. For some unknown and jarring reason they had been allowed to live. He listened intently, his ears combing over every sound, as he heard the heavy steps growing further and further away. When he could no longer hear the creature traveling, he stood and brought the unconscious man back to his shoulders.

It had begun to snow again. Unknown to Buchanan, this would be the final snow of this winter.

It was a heavy, wet snow. It didn't tumble from the sky. It dive-bombed from the heavens and found its frosted mount on clothes, twigs and hair. The last ditch effort of a vengeful winter. This storm was angry, and it gave every last bit of powder and cold that it had.

Snow clung to the men's faces as they trudged through the piling white, back to the splintered wood edifice that was Fort Preston.

Once, he had considered throwing together a torch and lighting it. But the glowing moon off the swirling snow provided adequate light, and led the way back to their cursed home.

The furious blizzard had twice turned them around and sent them wandering. But now, at long last, the open and welcoming arms of the gate appeared in the chaotic flurry.

Buchanan walked through the wooden opening that parted the white sea. He journeyed through, very attentive to the wavering unconsciousness of his cargo. Abraham was still far away, unaware.

This would suit nicely for their purposes.

Chapter 14

Abraham found himself outside the fort again, near the fictional lake that only existed in his slumbering hours.

Far away the boat was now, he could no longer see any of the passengers on the ghostly craft. He had given up on his fruitless screaming and instead opted to listlessly watch the glimmering light grow fainter and fainter, as it glided across the waters of the lake.

A hand on his shoulder. A comforting and warming hand that squeezed and lightly caressed his tired muscles. He turned, trying to ascertain the owner of the warmth.

Laura stood there, her face illuminated in a ghostly luminescence. She looked beautiful, as she always had. Her familiar features and comforting gaze were an agreeable sight in this repetitive, nightmarish dream-world.

"You look tired." Her voice played in his head, but her lips didn't part from their warm smile.

"I am." Abraham replied. "Don't know how much I've got left in me."

"You want to give up, to give in. But you can't." She said sadly.

"I miss you." He said to her mournfully.

She smiled more, her eyes softening up and looking at him with a loving gaze.

"I miss you too."

She drew something up in her hand and took his. She folded open his palm and placed something in it, something very small.

"You are so close to the end. You will have to fight hard to make it through."

Abraham looked down and opened in his hand. There, laying parallel with the lines on his palm; was a match. A single match and nothing else.

He looked up, not understanding. He opened his mouth to speak again, but Laura was gone. She was walking across the water toward the boat.

The boat was far out now, barely a white speck on the horizon. She shimmered across the water toward it incredibly fast, and was gone.

"I don't understand! Wait!" He tried to call out, but his voice was gone again.

Waves lapped against the banks of the phantom lake. Up and down, over and over. Soft rushes of water up the bank that lulled him into a feeling of peace.

Abraham opened his eyes slowly, the sound of the waves still semi-audible in his mind. He was incredibly sore and in tremendous pain, particularly in his stomach, shoulder and leg.

He looked around. He wasn't in the normal cabin, he was somewhere else. He realized that he was in the quarters that he had found the soldier's diary in. He lay on the bed, a cold cloth on his head and many quilts draped over him. At his side was a cup of water, he reached for it.

Shooting pain sent signals to his brain from all corners of his body. He fell back against the pillow and regrouped. Biting his lip in determination, he lifted himself again and barely managed to grab the cup before his muscles gave way and he fell back again.

He raised the cup above his prone body, raising his head again was out of the question. He tilted the cup and water ran out. Some landed in his open mouth and more splattered against his chin and neck. He gulped at the trickling stream greedily. When the cup had run dry and his shirt and blankets had been dampened with all of the missed water, he dropped the cup to his side and caved into the bed.

He was exhausted, bathed in all encompassing pain, and running a mean fever that he could feel coursing through him.

The door opened then. Buchanan walked through it and pulled a chair to the bedside. In his hands he held a bowl that steamed.

The smell of food pricked up Abraham's nose and he opened his eyes wider, tilting his head.

"Managed to bag a tiny rabbit this morning." Buchanan said as he fed a spoonful into Abraham's begging mouth.

Abraham swallowed past the pain in his burning throat. He opened his mouth for another bite and after he had downed it, he spoke. "How long have I been out?"

Buchanan fed him another spoonful and wiped his mouth for him. "Three days. I didn't think you'd make it through the first night. You were tore all to hell. I cleaned your wounds and dressed them, but I haven't managed to find any fresh clothes."

Abraham managed a weak nod. "Thank you. You saved my life Mr. Buchanan."

"Don't thank me yet. You've got a real screamer of a fever burning you up. You ain't out of the woods yet. Speaking of the woods... What the hell happened to you out there?"

Abraham swallowed some of the water that Buchanan had guided to his mouth.

"The Rogue." He replied before falling into a coughing fit.

Buchanan raised his eyebrows, impressed. "You're a tougher son of a bitch than I realized."

After he had stopped his coughing, Abraham looked to Buchanan again. "Where's Caleb?"

"Well." Buchanan started. "If you ain't realized it yet, you've got pneumonia to go with that fever. I thought it best to keep us separate from you, to limit the chances of infection."

Abraham nodded, a burning cough escaping him. "How is he?"

"Well enough." Buchanan replied. "Teased me to high hell over the pitiful size of this rabbit when he saw it."

Abraham smiled. "Good. That is good to hear."

Buchanan nodded, collecting his things and moving toward the door.

Abraham stopped him. "Buchanan."

The man turned just as he had reached the door. He walked back toward the bed.

"When you return, would you retrieve my journal? It's with my other things in the cabin. I'd like to write when I'm feeling better." Abraham asked.

Buchanan nodded. "Of course."

He turned again to walk toward the door.

It was then that Abraham noticed something that he hadn't before. "Are you limping?" He asked Buchanan.

Buchanan laughed and rubbed his leg. "Pulled the hell out of something in it. Dragging your mangy carcass through a blizzard was no easy task."

Abraham nodded, understanding.

"I'll be fine though. Takes a bit longer to heal the older you get." He opened the door and walked out.

Abraham looked at the warped wood of the door, thinking. Half of a thought had come and gone in his brain and he couldn't remember what it had been. After a moment, he brought his head back to the pillow and began to sleep.

Five days had passed.

Five days of Buchanan attending to the care and recovery of the ailing Abraham. He had changed the rags on his forehead and wiped sweat away. Had fed and watered him, and had assisted him with the bedpan when the need had arisen.

The fever had broken on the third day, and Abraham was relieved. The decent possibility of death temporarily put off, he had rested well and had grown stronger every day.

But still, the coughing fits of pneumonia had persisted. He could stand, could walk back and forth in the cabin but was still weak. He had gained a limp now. The torn tissue in his leg had healed irregularly and hurt when he walked.

Now, as he lay in bed, just having awoken this morning of the *sixth* day, he wrote in his journal.

Days have passed and I can feel my strength returning faster
than I expected.
The pain in my wounds diminishes by the hour.
Buchanan has offered great care and I look forward to seeing
Caleb again when this wretched cough diminishes. He has
recovered well, but I do not wish to endanger his recovery with a
bout of pneumonia.

Though there is something I must admit, something strange
persists in my brain regarding Buchanan.
Perhaps he is still spooked regarding the strange events we have
been witness to.
But he looks pale, sickly even, his eyes dart and he stares off for
long moments at a time.
Something in my intuition nags and worries me,

though I am in utter gratitude for him saving my life.

The snow has finally begun to melt ever so slowly,
and for once,
I see a light at the end of this misery.

Satisfied with the entry, Abraham closed the book and went to place it on the nightstand. The book missed and tumbled to the floor, bouncing under the frame of the bed.

"Dammit." Abraham muttered as he pulled himself from the bed and crouched down to retrieve it.

He felt something, a loose floorboard.

He vaguely recalled noticing it when the dynamite had terrifyingly tumbled from the shelf.

Now, he fiddled with it. He slipped one of his fingernails into the gap between boards and pulled up. The board came free and beneath it was a folded piece of paper, dirty and dingy from its hidden home.

Curious, he fetched the note from the floor compartment and replaced the board. He unfolded it and found that it was not a single piece, but several.

Several pages of manuscript, scribbled madly on both front and back. He shuffled through them for a moment and then sat on his bed to read.

The things attacked again last night. We did not lose anymore of our numbers but the few of us left, have grown weak.
I have decided to write down all that I have seen, all that I know, and all that I suspect.
I will write it and tell it all. To hell with the treason Mathers has threatened me with.
I will tell it all and will hide these pages where he will never suspect to find them and burn.
I will hide them under the floorboards in his quarters and I pray that someone someday will find it.
Someday someone will learn the shameful things that have taken place in this glorified coffin and this godforsaken land.

Intrigued, Abraham flipped the paper over and continued.

The start of our troubles began the day Mathers met with the tribal chief. He brokered the meeting between the army and the natives with a show of goodwill.
He lured the injuns here with an offering of molasses, tobacco and sugar. After they had taken the offering and agreed to the meeting, they arrived at the fort.

Instead of civil discussion, Mathers had the chief's two escorts hanged, and the chief himself, horsewhipped and thrown from the fort into the dirt.
When questioned about this atrocity, he simply said that he was "sending a message to any savages regarding his post."

After that day, the game all but vanished from the land. There was nary a squirrel to be hunted and our supplies of rations were running low. Any communication we would send out for aid would be killed. Injuns lurked behind every tree to put an arrow into any messenger's back that dared to run.

When Mathers decided the best course of action would be to wipe out the tribe altogether, a raiding party was mounted and set out. The injuns knew we were coming.
They led us into an infernal bog filled with parasites and mosquitoes. They hid in the shadows as we wandered the bog. They never even fired a single shot at us, they let us find our way out and leave.
They preferred to let us return to the fort and die of disease, spreading it to our comrades.
A fitting, and clever form of revenge from them I would suppose.

Weeks passed. Food ran out. We felled and devoured our horses. We boiled leather blankets and holsters. As time went on, death was lurking ever closer.

When the first man had finally dropped dead to the earth, the discussion happened. That stinking, diseased corpse lay upon the ground of the courtyard, and Mathers gathered us all around.

Thankfully, I do not remember the specifics of his speech other than "Let us partake of the meat God has provided for us."

I did not. I cast my portions into the shithouse. I was the only one who refused.

The others, the ones who partook, changed. Small differences at first. They were strong and looked incredibly healthy. But then, they would grow pale, look mad and ravenous.

Then, they would change.

When it was realized what was happening, one of the men closed his mouth around a pistol and fired. A moment later he resurrected, transforming and changing. It took ten men to wrestle him to the ground and burn him. That seemed to do the trick as his body did not reanimate again.

Those things. Those men.
They plague the forest now. They hunt and kill, and devour
without discretion.
I have come to accept that I will die here. I only wish that light
be shed upon the horror and atrocities that have taken place
here.

Abraham was thoroughly shaking now. He rifled through the pages. He found one, with a small section he hadn't read yet.

I am alone.
The last one left.
I hear them scratching at the walls now as the evening grows
darker. I will find somewhere to hide, and pray that they do not
find me.
It is all I can do now.
Hide. Hide and Pray.
Though, I feel certain that God has abandoned us.
This is the end.

Nathaniel Rodney Clifford

A chill went over Abraham. "Clifford?" He thought. "Wasn't that the name on the body in the closet?" He was certain it was, but didn't want to believe it.

The door began to open then, and while he didn't know why, he stuffed the notes under his pillow.

Buchanan entered, a small pile of wood in his arms. "Brought some more to stoke your fire with." He said and walked to the stove. He chucked in a couple logs and tended to the fire, poking and prodding it.

While Abraham watched him and considered telling him about the horrible tale he had just found, he saw something.

The side of Buchanan's pant leg was lightly stained with blood. Fresh blood that seeped from underneath.

Exertion can cause still healing stitches to weep. The labor of chopping wood had clearly made the knife wound from Caleb do the same thing.

Abraham's voice caught in his throat. He couldn't help but stare at it, trying to decide what it could mean. Fortunately, he managed to barely pull his eyes away when Buchanan stood up and dusted himself off.

Buchanan turned and looked at him. "Jesus, Mr. Mercer. You're as white as a sheet. Are you alright?"

Abraham brought himself to his senses and managed a believable nod. "I'm fine. Something in my stomach was turning for a moment, but I'm alright now."

Buchanan nodded and walked toward the door. "I'll be back with supper soon enough."

The door shut and Abraham was left in complete silence, aside from wind outside that creaked and howled. He was left to deliberate over the implications and the possible meanings of what he had just seen.

After working over the possibilities in his mind and weighing them individually, he knew what he had to do. He was going to see Caleb, see him with his own eyes. If Buchanan tried to stop him, he would knock him down.

He stood and creaked to the door. He carefully opened it and winced when it squeaked loudly.

He peered out of the slit in the door and saw Buchanan, at the far end of the courtyard chopping wood. Just as slowly, he closed the door again and went to get ready.

First, he put on his boots and found a scrap of cloth that would serve as a bandana. Then, he picked up different items in the room, weighing them in his hands.

His gun wasn't in here, and so something blunt and heavy would have to do.

There wasn't much of a variety of feasible choices.

A kettle? Too light.

A frying pan? Too awkward.

Finally, he settled on the fire poker Buchanan had been stirring the fire with, just a moment ago.

He picked it up and studied it, and then after a thought, stuck it back into the burning coals.

While the poker cooked, he crept to the door and peered out again.

Buchanan was still at the far end of the yard but was in the middle of one of his staring spells. He gazed off against the wood fence posts and stood limply.

Abraham swallowed and hoped that he had gotten the timing right. He pulled the bandana up and over his nose and walked back to the stove. He withdrew the poker and observed its dirty orange coloring. He could feel the heat radiating from it and held it carefully away from himself as he walked out.

Creeping out the door, with his fiery weapon at his side, he walked intently toward the other cabin. He walked briskly, trying his best not to drag his feet.

Gritting his teeth at the loud crunch of the frozen snow, he could see he was almost halfway across the courtyard. He hated this new limp and how slow it made him, but he pressed on, eyes locked on the door of the building.

"Mr. Mercer! Get back in your cabin!"

Abraham could almost hear his heart fall down into the deepest depths of his stomach. The hair-raising words had called from across the courtyard and were getting closer to him.

"Don't go in there!" The voice that was so close now called. "You get the boy sick, you'll both be ill and of no use to me!"

"I've covered my mouth!" Abraham called back, feigning nonchalance. "I just need to see him!"

"Soon enough!" Buchanan called, only feet away from him now. "But not yet. Go back to bed."

He was so close to the cabin now, another step or two and his fingers could grip the handle. He could rip the door open and see what lay on the other side.

The crunch of a footstep behind him.

Abraham turned and swung the fire poker through the air. Buchanan caught Abraham's arm mid swing and twisted his wrist.

So strong this man now was.

Buchanan, now in control of the hot weapon, pushed it downward and into Abraham's face. The red-hot metal landed in the middle of his eyebrow and crackled as it met live flesh.

Abraham screamed and tried to get away, but he was held tightly in this unbreakable grip. He could feel his flesh cracking and melting away, could smell the sickening stench of his own hair and flesh being cauterized into nothing.

He lashed out a foot, striking Buchanan in the wound on his leg. This made the grip relent enough for the fire poker to fall to the ground, sizzling as it met icy snow. Abraham jerked away and tried to grab the door again.

Buchanan was on him quickly. He grabbed Abraham around the waist and lifted him up. Spinning them both, he hurled Abraham through the air and onto his back.

Air rushed out of Abraham's lungs as his back met the frozen earth.

Buchanan was on top of him then.

He lashed out a dazed punch at his attacker and it met the man's cheekbone just below his eye.

Buchanan staggered a little bit but then looked at Abraham with a grin. He cocked back his own punch and delivered it savagely into Abraham's jaw, knocking him out cold.

Buchanan stood, dusting himself off. He walked to Abraham's legs, plucked one from the ground and began to drag him back to the cabin.

Chapter 15

Abraham's head bobbed and swayed as he navigated his way out of unconsciousness. His head throbbed and his face burned.

He felt his eyebrows wriggle as his face came back to life, and the burnt flesh cracked and rippled. The pain of that was enough to bring him out.

He was back in the second cabin. Not in his bed this time, but tied to a sturdy oak sitting chair.

Something was wrong with the chair, its wicker wrapped cushioning had been cut out and his ass hung out through the seat and into the air.

His arms and legs were firmly lashed to the solid supports and armrests. He tried to wiggle and rock the chair over, but it didn't budge. Even through the fog of sleep, he could see that the legs had all been driven to the floor with large nails.

"Oh Abraham." A voice spoke somewhere in the room. "You couldn't have heeded me could you? I did my best to make things agreeable."

Squinting to try and clear his vision, he could now see Buchanan was sitting on the bed opposite him. Abraham himself, was against the wall adjacent the door and held there firmly.

"Your bullheadedness is liable to get you killed one day. Better learn how to control that temper quick." Buchanan said coyly as he eyed the waking Abraham.

Abraham's face twisted into a menacing scowl. "What did you do to him?!" He shouted at the man on the bed.

Buchanan looked at the floor. Not in shame, but in thought. He looked more unhinged than ever. He was dirty, his hair fell down in unkempt whisps over his eyes. When he spoke, it sounded wrong. The spaces between his words rose and fell, and his sentences sounded jumbled and strange.

"The boy is dead. I suspect you know that." He sighed.

A pained whimper of anguish parted Abraham's lips and his head fell against his chest. He cried bitterly.

"But not by my hand." Buchanan continued.

"Oh, Horseshit!" Abraham shouted back, hot tears running down his cheeks. His face was scrunched tightly in anger, and the force of the muscles cracked the burned tissue that had slightly scabbed over. The wound wept pus and blood down into his vision, giving it a milky filter.

A million and one curses, insults, and promises of damnation exploded from Abraham's mouth as he berated the murderer that sat before him.

Buchanan allowed him to carry on for a moment, waiting for him to run out of breath. He raised a hand then, and quieted him slightly. "I can see why you would think that Abraham. But it ain't truth. It just ain't." He sighed through an inhale, and the sound was ghostly. "We're stuck here together. That's truth. So until your head has cooled, I'll stick with keeping you tied."

Abraham hissed an angry, mocking laugh. "Cool me all you want. The second I'm freed, I will kill you."

Buchanan rolled his eyes and nodded boringly. "I figured. But in the meantime, I'll keep you fed, watered and in otherwise good health." He gestured to the chair. "Hell, even when you get the call. I've fashioned that chair to open over a chamberpot beneath you." Buchanan grinned a little. "If'n you feel the need, give me a holler and I'll lower your britches for you."

Abraham swallowed all of this instruction with the enjoyment of bitter poison. He wanted to thrash around, to try and get out, but he knew that was pointless. He needed to save his strength, needed to think and to plan. He simply stared back at Buchanan.

After locking eyes for a moment further with Abraham, Buchanan stood and walked toward the door.

"I shall return with supper soon enough." He said with a parting glance to Abraham and exited the door and into the courtyard.

As the door closed behind him, Abraham loosed a horrible and shrieking cry of helplessness into the quiet cabin.

Laura had not come in his dreams again that night, though he had prayed that she would. He had not dreamt at all in fact.

After restless hours of writhing against the chair and his restraints without success, he had finally fallen asleep. A hollow, unrestful sleep that came only by default. Sleep that came with exhaustion, and ignored comfort.

Gradually then, he began to wake. The comforting nothingness of waking was quickly ripped from him as he found himself still in this nightmare. Tied to a chair and at the mercy of a madman.

Hours passed without Buchanan coming to call, and Abraham was met with another horrible thought, aside from his current captivity.

What if Buchanan died?

It didn't matter how. All that would matter was that he could not escape. He would gradually starve to death, and rot in this chair as time marched on. He would be given no window, no lapse of judgment from Buchanan where he could possibly break free.

He would sit, would soil himself eventually, and would sit in his own filth until he finally withered away.

In the midst of this thought, Buchanan entered with a fresh bowl of stew in his hands. He whistled casually, as if he were moseying into work ten minutes late. He set down the stew next to Abraham; who refused to even so much as meet his gaze.

"Snow seems to have finally called it quits for the winter." Buchanan remarked in a friendly manner.

Abraham didn't acknowledge this remark, but he did agree with it. Even though he hadn't set foot outside since Buchanan had knocked him out, he had heard water dripping from the roof of the cabin during the warmer parts of the day.

Spring had finally begun to stir from its long slumber and it would soon wake, driving the last bones of winter away until next year.

Buchanan picked up the bowl of stew and sat down across from Abraham, just far enough away to be cautious.

He served up a spoonful and extended it toward Abraham's tightly shut mouth.

"Here." He said, hovering the spoon in front of Abraham.

The captive man jerked his head away and said nothing.

Buchanan sighed softly and dropped his head. "Come on now. How ever will you kill me if you don't maintain your strength?"

Abraham's lip quivered and a single tear crested his eye before tumbling down his cheek. His stomach growled and he hated that it did. Angrily, he relented and opened his mouth, accepting the food.

Buchanan grinned and fed Abraham another. "Thank you Mr. Buchanan. Without you I would surely be resigned to chewing boot leather." Buchanan spoke to himself.

Another bite of food and more words from Buchanan.

"Well, Mr. Mercer. I am happy to be of assistance. How is the food?" He asked himself.

"A little better than a kick in the teeth." Buchanan continued in a parody of Abraham's voice. "But given the circumstances I cannot complain."

When the bowl had run dry, Buchanan dabbed at Abraham's lips with a rag. He held it carefully, ready to dart away should Abraham try to bite one of his fingers off. After he had cleaned the man, he gathered his things and began to leave.

"Good day Mr. Mercer." Buchanan said with a nod of his head.

Abraham stopped him, shame lighting his cheeks. He kept his head low as he spoke. "Wait." He breathed.

Buchanan spun around, eyebrows raised. "Yes?" He asked.

Sheepishly and not wanting to say the words, Abraham murmured. "I have to..." He cleared his throat. "I have to relieve..."

Buchanan replied loudly, feigning annoyance. "You'll have to speak up!"

"I have to relieve myself!" Abraham shouted back, embarrassed.

Buchanan smiled a toothy grin. "Well why didn't you just say so?" He replied back cheerily.

A sickening feeling of humiliation burned in Abraham's chest and cheeks, as Buchanan set down his things and lowered himself to assist him. He shuddered, cringing with shame to himself as his pants were pulled down by Buchanan.

"Go on then." Buchanan said. "I won't watch you."

Restrained relief, mixed with the disgust of this indignity crossed Abraham's face, as the bedpan filled up beneath him.

Moments later, Buchanan was returning his pants to their previous position and leaving with the bedpan.

"I ain't gonna wipe your ass for you." Was all Buchanan offered before leaving Abraham to wallow in his thoughts.

Abraham spent the next several hours drifting in and out of consciousness. Sometimes he would sleep a little, other times he would stare off in a daydream. Either would usually end the same way. He would awake violently, screaming and shaking.

But most of the time he just sobbed.

On one of these jolts back into reality, his leg had thrashed wildly and met something sharp. Something that dug into his leg and scratched it deeply.

He could feel blood leaking down his leg, but he didn't care. He wanted to know what he had just happened upon below his waist.

He couldn't see over his knees, and could only guess as he lifted his leg up and sideways to feel it.

As good as he could figure, one of the nails had been driven into the leg a little sideways. The head of it had been bent and was quite sharp.

He allowed himself the faintest glimmer of a smile. He raised his leg again, and felt the rope catch on the sharp edge. A little too eagerly, he pushed down against it and the grip of the nail slipped. Instead of cutting the rope, another deep cut sliced into his leg.

He bit his tongue in pain, as he felt more blood slithering down his ankle. More careful this time, he brought his leg up again. He felt the rope catch and began to go up and down in a sawing motion.

He had managed three or four good passes and had begun to fray the rope. But then, with a slightly incorrect motion, he slipped again and slashed his leg over the same spot.

"Goddammit!" He shouted, slamming his head into the wall behind him in anger.

Buchanan came through the door then. Abraham jumped and quickly tried to compose himself. He stared at Buchanan, who now by all accounts was looking remarkably more terrible.

Pronounced veins on his neck had begun to bulge under his pale and seemingly paper thin skin. His eyes were a jaundice yellow, with nothing much behind them.

He didn't say anything, he just stared at Abraham with his mad and wild eyes.

An unwilling participant in this staring contest, Abraham shouted at the lumbering guard. "Say something! Say something Goddammit!"

Buchanan did not.

He sniffed lightly, the aroma of iron partially in the air. He looked down and saw a pool of blood forming around Abraham's foot. He crouched and lifted the pant leg that hid the wound.

He sighed and slapped the wound viciously. Abraham jumped back in the chair from the jolt of pain.

Buchanan looked at the nail, still wet with blood. He stood and placed his boot heel on it. Using his body weight, he bent the nail about three inches away from Abraham, making it now out of his reach entirely.

Stumbling, like a drunk, Buchanan exited the door and into the courtyard.

From the looks of the pale gray light outside, it was either early morning or late evening. Abraham had lost all sense of time and didn't know the week, let alone the hour.

He knew that if he didn't think of something new to try, and fast, he may lose his mind entirely.

He could, in all likelihood, be reduced to a babbling lunatic, the next time Buchanan decided to pay him a visit. He struggled against the bonds again and tried to focus on where they were holding him.

He began to realize that he could feel the bonds on his wrists stop on the protruding bone of his thumb. The rope would catch right where it connected on the joint, and would make escape impossible.

And just like that, he suddenly had a small semblance of a plan. Though this plan he did not like, not at all.

Outside, at the chopping block, as he had been for many days now, Buchanan sat. Tooling the ax around in his hands, he stared off into nothing.

The broadcast had long since been dormant. Or, it may have just struggled to get through, in this decaying mortal shell of the mad man. Either way, it came through now, loud and clear.

"Finish it. Come home."

Abraham used his chin to bunch up his shirt around his neck. He opened his mouth and took a large piece of fabric in between his teeth, biting down hard on it. With what was coming next, he did not need half of a tongue to go with it.

Leaning up and forcing his hand under his ass as best he could, he extended his thumb and pushed on it awkwardly. He could feel the bone questioning him as he did this, uncomfortable with the unnatural angle he was forcing it to travel.

He eased some more of his weight down onto the thumb. What was at first mild discomfort, was growing into a more nagging and prevalent pain. He could feel his tendons and bone crying out at him to cease with this foolishness.

It was now or never.

Abraham dropped his entire body weight onto the bent thumb. He felt it snap with a crack that shook up his arm and into his brain.

He screamed, the sound muffled by the mouthful of fabric. Tears welled in his eyes and his hand throbbed angrily.

After he had fought through the initial shock of the obliterating pain, he forced himself to sit up again and draw his thumb out from under him.

The finger was hanging limply and wouldn't hardly move when he tried.

"Let's hope that this actually works." Abraham thought to himself before he lowered his hand and began to pull up against the rope.

The rough fibers of the rope burned and scratched at the skin on his wrist as he pulled. He felt the limp thumb push into the flesh of his palm and relent against the rope. Wriggling and bucking, he finally managed to pull the hand free.

He stifled a triumphant and squeaky yelp and went to work immediately on his other hand.

Buchanan sat still at the chopping block, the ax held tightly in his hands.

He was receiving his final transmission. A general, thanking a soldier for a job well done, and sending him on one final mission with a one way ticket.

He stood, ax dropping and dragging next to his feet. He lumbered forward and began to walk toward the cabin.

If one were to observe the tracks left by Buchanan on this final march, they might picture the strange mental-image of a snake slithering alongside a man as if they were old friends. Buchanan's bootprints trudged along the dirty slush and his ax dragged lazily, this way and that beside him, leaving a snail trail in the snow. His companion on this final quest; a deadly serpent.

He had almost reached the door and had brought the ax up from its serpentine travels. He now held it, two handed, ready to strike.

Then, from out behind the cabin, something slammed into him, knocking him down to the ground with a thud.

The shock of the blow and the haze of his decomposing humanity slowed Buchanan's response.

He tried to turn and look. But before he could see the fire poker that was lodged deep into his ribcage, Abraham had snatched the knife that Buchanan wore on his leg.

Buchanan, with his yellowed and bloodshot eyes could only just barely see the glint of the knife in the early morning sun. The shine of the blade winked at him, as it was plunged sharply into his chest.

He jolted from the force of the blow and gasped. He coughed, blood rising in his mouth and choking him.

Abraham raised the knife again and brought it down into Buchanan's windpipe. The dying man gurgled and spasmed, as the remaining sliver of light left his eyes.

In these actions, so sudden and violent, John Buchanan was finally dead.

Abraham sucked in grateful and adrenaline filled breaths. He sucked in the fresh air of the morning as if it were his last. He shouted to the heavens in victory and beat his chest like an ape.

He looked at Buchanan's corpse and spit upon it. He looked at the hollow eyes of this monster.

He really looked at him.

Jesus Christ, he looked terrible. He was gaunt, almost emaciated. Veins spiraled down from his scalp that had lost large clumps of hair. His fingernails were unkempt, caked with dirt and incredibly sharp. His lips were gnawed and nearly chewed off. His dead stare looked to the ever-brightening sky in a limp, vacant gaze.

Though he didn't know why, his mind flashed to the pages in the floorboards. Abraham shook off this thought and gathered himself to his feet. He limped toward the cabin, one arm hanging at his side.

He came to the door and held the handle steadily for a moment. He knew Caleb was dead. But some part of him hoped that when he threw open the door, he would find him sleeping peacefully on the bed.

The door creaked open as he pulled with his good hand. Sadly, all he was given to look at, was the tattered and somber interior of the completely empty cabin.

He didn't enter, he didn't bother. He let the door go and it swung shut on its hinges. If he could help it, it would be the last time he ever looked at the inside of that cabin again. He leaned his head against the door and breathed quietly.

Then, as his gaze was cast downward, he caught a glimpse of the slightest remainder of blood on the ground.

He raised his head and looked more closely at it. He scanned around and found another, then another. He followed this trail of blood around the far wall of the cabin.

When he rounded the corner to the small space between it and the perimeter wall, he fell to his knees at the shock of what he saw.

Blood.

So much frozen blood was splashed and soaked into every square inch of the ground. It caked the fence and back wall of the cabin.

His cold hand thrust itself against his burning forehead and Abraham collapsed onto the ground. His back fell against the fence, and he slid down it, hyperventilating hysterically.

He spoke. He shouted at the cold wind that filled the fort. "Buchanan!" He howled into the freezing air. "Buchanan what did you do!!?"

His eyes burned and his chest heaved. Left with all of this shattered existence, this bald-faced misery, he could only bury his head in his hands and sob.

A deafening crash.

Something had smashed through the gate so fiercely, that it had knocked it off of its hinges completely and broke it entirely.

Abraham jumped to his feet, running purely on adrenaline and instinct. When he came out from the small alley between the cabin and the wall, the first thing he saw was that Buchanan was gone.

He doubletaked over to the blood soaked impression in the snow, where the body had been just a moment before. Stumbling in a wandering and empty daze, Abraham went to where the man had died.

Hand prints, boot prints, and scrambling motions of limbs were reflected in the snow.

Somehow, the obviously dead body of Buchanan had reanimated and fled. With all that he had been subjected to, his mind couldn't give it much more consideration than that.

He looked closely at the ground and followed the tracks. They were close together at first, stumbling and awkward. Then, the tracks were strong, determined.

Out of the corner of his eye, he spotted the obliterated remnants of Buchanan's boots that had been cast aside from his path.

Then, something different, something strange. The bare footprints that led away from the boot remnants, gradually changed. They morphed with each step that advanced on the gate. They transformed into something else entirely, something familiar.

The tracks that the creatures had left.

Abraham stopped, staring at the horribly recognizable print. He looked up to the decimated gate and back to the print.

This was too much. Head in his hands and swirling with a million thoughts, Abraham stumbled to the side of the courtyard fire pit.

There, he sat.

He sat there a long time.

In the empty shell of a broken and hollow man, his brain tried to operate, it tried to compute. He could not begin to understand how what he was *coming to understand* could possibly be.

It all connected. The diary, the creatures in the woods, and the unhingement of Buchanan.

Except, it didn't. Not entirely.

Until it did.

Abraham had been fixating on something in the fire. An oddly shaped, black rock that sat in the center of the fluttering ash and coals.

But it wasn't a rock.

There, in the center of the glowing embers of Buchanan's last fire, was a skull. Caleb's skull.

Then, it connected.

Abraham fell to his knees and vomited onto the snow. He heaved until his guts had been fully and totally purged. Purged of any remnants of the boy who had once been his friend.

The boy that he had watched with amusement and pride as the wagon train traveled. The boy that had made his wife smile and laugh, up until she died.

The boy that Buchanan had fed him, disguised as a rabbit stew.

His thoughts traveled one way, and then another. But ultimately they all guided him to look upon his hands. He already knew what he would see.

Just as Buchanan's skin had grown, Abraham's hands had become pale. His fingernails were getting sharp, and pronounced veins were beginning to bulge through his translucent skin.

He shrieked. He howled as the last remnants of his fragmenting mind scattered, dancing away into oblivion.

Then, when he finally felt he would collapse into the void and lie motionless on the snow until he finally died, a voice spoke to him.

Not a voice, but a memory of one.

"You are so close to the end. You will have to fight hard to make it through."

Laura's words in his dreams.

Except it didn't make any sense. What end? This horrible end of collapsing into madness and freezing to death?

There was nothing.

There was nothing he could do. He was resigned to die and could not be persuaded otherwise.

Then, far away and distantly on the wind, he heard it.

Singing. Yes, singing.

A chorus of voices he had heard for months. Singing hymns and carrying on, as their wagons traveled west. Familiar voices of men, women and children singing in unison. Heartily and without concern for pitch or melody, a mass gathering of voices sang hymns as they traveled onward.

It was Clanton.

It was Clanton and the whole Goddamn Jacobs-Clanton handcart company. That cowardly bastard Elliot had lied.

How could they not have seen that?

They all had known the behavior and trappings of a coward. But they hadn't considered for even a moment that he had lied? That they all were basking in this personal hell only miles from their friends and tribe?

That was the end. That was the reason.

They were headed right here and into these woods. The fort was broken, the gate unsecured. Come nightfall, the creatures would tear them apart.

Hell, if his own transformation worked quickly enough, Abraham might even be the one to do the tearing.

"But how am I supposed to change that?" Abraham thought frantically.

"What am I supposed to do?!" He shouted out into the wind.

He remembered the match. The single match that Laura had given him. At first he didn't understand, but then it came to him.

He shook his head.

There was no reason to believe that it would work. The dynamite they had buried so long ago would be wet. It wouldn't work.

But it would, it would still be good. He knew it and knew that it couldn't be any other way.

He knew that if he followed the ragged footprints of what was once Buchanan, he could find where they spent their days. He could find their home, their nest, and blow it to high-hell.

He stood then. Shaking and weak, yet determined. He would end it once and for all. He would purge these woods of the abominations that had taken root here. He would have to fight hard to make it through, but he would damn sure try.

He had walked out of the gate, turned around, and taken one last look at the place where the thread had caught, and the entire spool of yarn had unraveled.

The skeleton of the fort looked back at him as he left. This unholy monument of obscenity and atrocity watched, as its final guest disappeared into the woods.

Chapter 16

It had taken him much less time than he had expected. He had found Clifford's remains and the dynamite quite easily. Buchanan's tracks led him right to them and continued on past it.

He crouched, digging through frozen snow to the dynamite parcel that slept dormantly underneath.

When he had found it, the soggy cloth worried him about the feasibility of this plan. When he unwrapped the cloth and pulled forth the first stick, his hopes almost departed entirely.

The first charge of dynamite was soaked through, with its paper wrapping flaking away. But, beneath the first charge, the other two sticks were not completely dry, but not terribly damp either.

They would have to do.

He placed the ruined charge back down, next to Clifford and carefully wrapped up the remaining two.

He stood and gave a nod of thanks to the old bones that had watched over his final stand. Looking down and finding Buchanan's tracks again, he resumed following them.

Not even one hundred feet from where the dynamite had been, he found the nest. A large opening, maybe six feet in diameter was tucked between two hefty boulders at the top of a small embankment.

Staring at the dark entrance with wild images dancing in his mind about what might lay beyond, he shivered. He suddenly wished he had brought a lantern and cursed himself that he hadn't.

Setting down the parcel of explosives, he retrieved a partially dry, wooden stick from nearby. He pulled off his coat and the shirt underneath, wincing at the chill of the air on his bare flesh. Using his mouth to hold the stick, to make up for his broken thumb, he wrapped the shirt tightly around it.

Without fuel to soak it in, he would not have long before the torch died. He would also have to watch the burning flame carefully. If it dripped and landed on the dynamite before he got far enough in, it would be curtains before the end of the show.

He withdrew a book of matches from his discarded coat and frowned at the remaining two that looked back at him.

He struck the first match and cursed loudly a moment later when the wind blew it out.

Carefully this time, he struck another and did not withdraw his hand away until the torch had lit completely. He stood again, bare chested and freezing in the air. One hand held the burning torch and the other the parcel of dynamite, tucked under his arm with the limp thumb.

Abraham Mercer took his first step into the complete and terrifying black.

"And into the vastness of the night we shall venture." He thought passively as he stepped carefully down the steep and rocky burrow.

The thing that really struck him as he navigated this dank and freezing cave, was the absence of any form of life. No rats scurried away from his blazing flame, no snakes either. No spiders or webs alighting on the ceiling, not even any frozen earthworms lying in the loose soil.

The long and winding caverns of this earthen burrow were confusing, and he was sure at least twice that he had gotten lost.

But then, he found it. He found them all.

A winding curve of the nest brought him into a large circular section, and into the center of the entire hive. There were nearly a hundred of them, slumbering in scattered groups all over the ground of this bunker.

At one point, as he cast a waving glance over the slumbering creatures, he half-thought he saw Buchanan, but thought better of going back to confirm.

They looked peaceful, cozy in this dank cavern. His fear and apprehension had begun to melt away as he looked at them. He didn't feel disgust, he felt camaraderie in some low and animalistic part of his brain, a brotherhood. He was changing rapidly and he didn't actually know if he wanted to go through with it.

Then he saw her. Not Laura, but still her.

A faint, glowing orb stared back at him from the other side of the sleeping ghouls. He felt his mind right itself and he looked down at the wrapping tucked under his arm.

Nodding to himself, he walked toward the center of the room, stepping carefully over the unconscious creatures. He placed the parcel on the ground and hovered his dying torch over it.

He looked up to the glowing orb once again and smiled sadly. "I'm coming home."

He held the torch to the parcel, waiting for it to dry the damp fabric and light. The old withered cloth lit moments later and he watched it intently, worrying about whether or not it would work.

An explosion, though muffled by layers of earth, echoed loudly throughout the entire forest.

Inside the nest, the few creatures that weren't instantly shredded by the force of the blast, were quickly buried under thousands of pounds of crumbling dirt and rock.

The home of these unholy abominations was brought to a pile of smoking rubble in mere seconds. The great and spacious hive had been pulled down, and the earth salted.

Far back up the trail, through the winding deer paths and through the pines, over boulders and rocks, babbling brooks and freezing creeks; Fort Preston stood.

The frozen and abandoned structure was left deserted in the icy wilderness and it would never have anyone stay within its walls again.

Epliogue

When Father Clanton and the surviving members
of the Jacobs-Clanton Handcart Company had come upon
the yawning gates of Fort Preston, they had stopped. They
searched the fort and had found many unsettling things
within.

After, a large meeting was held to discuss what
should be done next. When the meeting had concluded, it
was unanimously decided that none of the parties involved
would ever speak of what might have transpired behind the
ghostly walls of the fort ever again.

It was also decided that the route would be diverted
south and toward the border of the territories of Utah and
Arizona.

They would find their Zion. A term that Clanton
had adopted after conversing and trading with the
Mormon settlers they had encountered as they journeyed
south through Utah.

As it turns out, the Zion of The Jacobs-Clanton
handcart company would be just over the line, and into the
territory of Arizona.

Mercy was what they called their little township. A small strip of desert land in a nondescript valley.

Though the winters were cold, and the summers sweltering, they were glad that heavy snow was not a regular occurrence in their new home. They had seen too much of it in their time, and wished never to see it again.

Through many hard years, the town grew into a respectable and well traveled stop on the route for miners and railroad workers alike.

But ultimately, as many small towns do, the place was eventually left abandoned and later demolished, nearly seventy-five years later, when the property was purchased by a private developer.

Fort Preston sat abandoned for many years until it was finally destroyed in 1955. It had long since fallen into a state of unsalvageable disrepair, and had little more than deer wandering its courtyard in all those years since Abraham Mercer's final stand.

When the property was finally purchased, the wrecking crew that pulled the old bones of the fort down, would not find anything remarkable about the event.

Time marches on and time forgets.

Acknowledgements

Thank you for taking the time to read this story. I hope you enjoyed reading it as much as I enjoyed telling it. I'd like to thank my friends Shane, Shytei and Ayden for encouraging me into turning one of my favorite screenplays I've written, into one of my now favorite books.

I'd also like to thank my friend and fellow book nerd; Corbyn Alvey, for rekindling my love of books and allowing me to bounce ideas off of him in the late hours of the night.

Wow, two spooky westerns in a row. I'm gonna have to try something different for my next one.

Printed in Great Britain
by Amazon

77534352R00174